Sebastian Gerald

Berkley's Bastards Book 5

KATHI S. BARTON

This is a work of fiction. Names, characters, places, and incidents are products of the author's imagination or are used fictitiously and are not to be construed as real. Any resemblance to actual events, locations, organizations, or persons, living or dead, is entirely coincidental.

World Castle Publishing, LLC
Pensacola, Florida
Copyright © 2023 Kathi S. Barton
Paperback ISBN: 9798891260986
eBook ISBN: 9798891260993
First Edition World Castle Publishing, LLC, November 6, 2023
http://www.worldcastlepublishing.com
Cover: Karen Fuller
Editor: Karen Fuller

Prologue

Toby cleaned off the bar while watching the game on the big screen. It was the best seat in the house unless you were at the game, she thought. While she didn't love being a bartender, she did enjoy the perks of it. Games with people she knew. Snacks as much as she wanted and a beer on occasion when it was a great game. The door opened down from her, and she watched as a man walked in and sat at the bar. Making her way toward him, she was surprised at how handsome he was. Not only that but since he was sitting on a barstool, he was as tall as her six foot one inches.

"What can I get you?" He said a beer and a burger. Well done, too. "Fries? Or tater salad. Or both. It's late, so they'll be throwing it out at the end of the shift anyway since it's Saturday."

"Both?" Nodding, she made her way to the kitchen. Sammy said he'd get it right up, and she pulled his beer. They had it on tap so she could watch the game that was going on while she did it. Taking him his beer, he asked her if she knew someone named Anderson. "I'm on my way to finding him around here."

"First or last name?" He grinned and told her last. "There's a couple here named Anderson. They're an older couple."

"No, this guy would be about my age. Late twenties to early thirties. I don't know what he does or what he looks like." Toby didn't know why, but she felt alarms go off in her head. There was no way that this guy was in his late twenties to early thirties. She'd put him more at the top of being in his early fifties. There was graying at his temples, for Christ's sake. "I think he's married, though. Does that help?"

"Can't say that I know anyone that fits that. You can ask around to the others here if you want. But I don't know." Instead of chatting it up as she usually did, she started away. When he grabbed her arm, she looked at his hand on her. "You will remove your hand from me, or I'm going to hurt you."

"For detaining you?" She only nodded but didn't move. "I want you to tell me all you know about the man that you're lying to me about. He's looking for his half-brother, and you'll tell me what you know. Now, kid or else."

"You don't want to talk to me in that tone, shithead. I'm a good deal smarter and stronger than I look. Remove your hand, or I will. You doing it will save you time in the emergency department." Instead of letting her go, he squeezed just a bit harder. Knowing that she was going to be carrying a bruise for a while, she smiled at him. "You were warned."

By the time the ambulance arrived, she was serving up more beers. The one that the stranger ordered was eaten by Columbus, the old man who sat in the bar only to watch the game with them. The police arrived not five minutes later. They were usually quick to respond when she called, as she handled most of the rowdy customers when necessary. Officer Bentley, the new guy on the force, was with the second cruiser. He asked her what happened.

"He touched me when I didn't allow it." He looked at the man on the floor and then back at her. "I warned him to let me go. More than I do for other patrons that come in here. But he gave me the jitters. Also, he threatened me with telling him something about your friend."

"Which one?" She told him, and he asked her what he wanted. "I mean, did he seem the type that — nah, he didn't want money. What did he want, Toby?"

"He was looking for someone that was half-brother to him. He didn't give me a name, but like I said, he gave me the jitters and then threatened me." Again, she looked at the man on the floor and then back at him. "I don't give someone a fighting chance to hurt me again. They must have told you that about me."

"They did. But I was just thinking of how much strength it might take a person to remove someone's arm with a hatch. No offense, but someone as slim and small built as you would have to have a hidden strength you don't let someone see." She told him that looks can be deceiving. "They certainly can. I'm going to call my brother. I know you're going to be closing up soon. Can you wait for him?"

"Sure. I'm off tomorrow and Monday. I don't mind waiting around." The game ended with their team winning. Another football game in the pocket.

Soon after that, most of the patrons left, Columbus leaving her a big tip when he went out the door. The police were talking to them about what had happened. As it turned out, no one knew that she'd dealt with the man until he hit the floor screaming. They still paid little attention to him as their team was in the in-zone.

Caleb showed up about twenty minutes after two. It was then that she noticed that there was a man in the back that hadn't left. When Caleb shook her hand, the man ambled, no other word for it, to where they were standing. It took her less time than it had Caleb to realize that the man could have been his twin.

Once they hugged, big bear hugs like large men were apt to do, she watched as they sobbed over each other. When Harlin was called in, the three of them talked all over each other while they got acquainted. She went to the back room to rotate some stock that she had planned on doing in the morning.

"Toby?" She came out of the walk-in just as Harlin joined her in the back room. It was a quarter past three now, and she was suddenly feeling her long day. "I'm so sorry about this. We got to talking and lost track of time. This is the man that the other man was looking for."

"Yeah, I figured at much." She locked the walk-in up and moved to the front of the bar. "I'm exhausted, so if you guys wouldn't mind saving this until the morning, I'd greatly appreciate it."

"What time is good for you?" She said that she didn't sleep much, so she could be ready around seven-thirty. "How about we meet at my house and — no, that won't work. I don't have any furniture yet. Caleb's home. We'll all meet there and have some breakfast. Is that all right?"

"Yeah, sure. I'll just need an address." He gave it to her, and she made a mental note of it. "Great. I don't know what else I can tell you other than what I already did, but I'll come over."

When they left, she locked up the bar and made her way out to her car. She was surprised to find another car in the lot other than hers and the man that she'd hurt. When someone stepped out, she pulled her gun and nearly fell to the ground when Harlin said it was him.

"Christ, I could have killed you, you fucking idiot. Who gets out of a car in the fucking dark? You don't do that or someone might put a bullet in your head. Next time, think." He laughed and told her how sorry he was. "Yeah, sure. Now, why are you here?"

"We wanted to make sure that you were all right when you left." She asked him if she looked like she was unprepared for shit like someone sneaking up on her. He laughed again. "No, as a matter of fact, you look like you could take on the world. But we did want to make sure that you got in your car safely. The police will be coming for the man's car sometime tomorrow. I wanted to let you know that, too."

"Thanks. I have a standing order with the police to make sure that any cars left on the lot for more than twenty-four hours they're to be towed." He told her that was a good idea. "Thanks. I do have them on occasion."

"What do you do? I know that you're more than a bartender. You have skills that I've only noticed tonight. You've been in the service, I think." She didn't answer him. "Or not. You don't have to answer. But I will tell you that my sister-in-law and Caleb have connections that can find out almost anything."

"They'll be wasting their time." She nodded toward her car. "I'm out of here. If you think of anything else tonight, just make a note and ask me tomorrow. I'm dead, standing on my feet right now. And don't sneak up on me again. It will get you dead."

She made her way to her car while he was still laughing. The moron was going to get himself dead if he wasn't careful. Toby noticed that they followed her home, too. She did wonder what they'd think about her house. It was fucking huge, but it was all hers.

Going into her home, she didn't bother turning to see if they left. Once she was inside, she kicked off her boots and made her way to the kitchen. As usual, there were sandwiches left in the fridge for her, and she pulled the plate out and ate one of them standing at the counter. When she was finished with the second one, she sat down at the table and read the notes that had been left for her to go over.

"There you are." Toby smiled at Ginger, the cook and chief of her home. "I thought you'd been hurt. Where have you been, young lady? Getting laid, I hope."

"Yes, by six men. It wasn't as fun as I thought it would be." She tsked at her. Then told her what had happened. "I'm having breakfast with Caleb Anderson in the morning. I'm not going to bother going to sleep now, but I'll take a nap when I get home. Have you been waiting up for me? I asked you not to do that."

"I have to keep an eye on you. It was a promise I made, and you know it." Ginger told her that she was sorry. "I shouldn't have said that. But I did make a promise, and I intend to keep it. How much do they know about you, honey?"

"I guess they'll do a background check. They won't find anything, but they'll do it. Other than what I want them to find anyway." Ginger told her that she'd make her some juice. "No, don't do that. I'm going to go and work in my office for a little while. You go back to bed. Since I won't be here, you should sleep in. Maybe have a little fun with Herman when you guys wake up."

"You little turd." She was still laughing when she made her way to her office. Toby was wide awake now and didn't think that she'd even shut her eyes.

She was so hyped up right now. As she turned on her computer, she thought of what the Andersons would find.

They'd find that her parents were dead, as well as her grandma. Grandda was still around, but he wasn't ready to face the world. He told her since the love of his life was gone. She also knew that they'd find that she was wealthy, but not anything about amounts. It cost her a great deal of money and time to make sure that no one other than her attorney knew her net worth.

There were little things, too, that they'd find out. Like she'd been a child prodigy. But nothing to the extent of how smart she was. Nor would they find out that she had several doctorates, all of them that had served her well over her young life. At only twenty-seven, she was about as educated as anyone could ever be.

Finishing up on her computer, she closed things down and went to her room, the one that she'd been in since she'd been a child, and took a shower. After getting dressed, she was out the door at a little after seven. There was a limo in her drive that she didn't recognize but didn't draw her gun, waiting to see who might pop out.

"You were right." She told Harlin that she normally was. "Good to know. But we didn't find out much about you. But Tabby, Caleb's wife, is making another call now, so who knows. Caleb has been making notes since we left you. I have a feeling that you didn't sleep either."

"I don't sleep much." When she got into the car with him, he told her that he had checked in on the man; the name on his driver's license said he was Richard Weed. She laughed. "So his name is Dick Weed, is it?" It took Harlin a few seconds to get what she said, and he laughed as well.

"I guess I'm too sleep-deprived, or I might have gotten that sooner." The drive to the house was smooth. She had a limo as well but rarely rode in it anymore. She much preferred to drive herself. Unless it was something important that she had to attend. "This is what we were able to find on you."

Toby didn't bother taking the sheet of paper. "I know what you were able to find. The rest is personal." He nodded and put the paper on the seat between them. "What's the big deal about knowing anything about me? It's not like we're going to be besties, is it? I mean, I've lived in this town all my life and have never once run into any of you."

"I don't know. Honestly, I have no idea. I think that Caleb wants it because he feels like he owes you. And he did mention and discarded that you could have been with Dick Weed in some way. Like I said, he discarded that idea right away." She didn't bother saying anything because there was nothing to say to him about it. "You have money. And pardon me for saying it, but I'd say that you have a great deal of it."

"I do." Nothing more from either of them on that. "That man, the stranger that is related to the three of you, he's a hard man. Just by the little bit that I saw of him, I'd say that he's got nightmares that even nightmares would have bad dreams about."

"I didn't catch that. But then I was so happy that he'd made it to us." She looked out the window when the limo stopped. "This is Caleb's house. The entire family is here, including my wife, to meet you. Like I said, they're thrilled that you were able to save our brother."

She didn't want to meet the family and didn't think that she had anything to say to a bunch of strangers. But she was here now and was going to make the best of it. It wasn't until she was being introduced to Tabby Anderson that she saw someone that she knew.

"Gracie?" she was engulfed in strong arms in that second. While she was babbling about how long it had been since she'd seen her, Toby just let her. One thing that she remembered about Gracie was that she would wind down soon. "You're married now? That's wonderful."

"I can't believe you're here. I mean, I heard that your parents were gone. And your grandma. My goodness, you look so much like her. But I think that the last I heard, you were still—" She cut her off. "I'm sorry. I do tend to forget that part."

Toby could tell that everyone was curious, but she nor Gracie would say anything. As they were headed to the big living room—breakfast was still a bit away yet—they talked about the bar incident. She told them the same thing that she'd told the police last night and waited for the questions. There were plenty of those as well.

When they were told that breakfast was ready, they stopped all talk about anything to do with the bar and any business that might have come up. They simply enjoyed the meal and the light conversation. Just as she was finishing up, a little boy came and crawled up on her lap. She was told his name was George. They stared at each other for several seconds before he finally laid his head on her chest and closed his eyes.

"I'm not all that good with kids." Yazzie, his mother, said that he wasn't all that good with adults other than family. "I'm not family. Why did he pick me?"

"I'm sure that he saw something in you that he

wanted to help you with. I've noticed that about him. He is quick to come to someone when they need a hug." She didn't think that she needed a hug but didn't say anything. "If you're ready, we can tell you what we've been able to find out about Dick Weed."

~*~

Sebastian watched the woman as she spoke to the others. He'd noticed when he'd seen her last night that she was comfortable with herself. In her own skin, he'd heard people say. Not only that, but he was also able to tell that she'd not felt any remorse about killing Dick either. He had died last night from blood loss.

"You said that you lived here all your life. How come we never crossed paths before this?" She asked Caleb if he meant because they were in the same social circles. "No. I didn't mean that at all. I've lived here for less than a year now, and I doubt very much there has been an occasion for us to be at anything that would have social standards. You need to get the chip off your shoulder and let us be friends."

"No offense, Caleb, but I'm not good around people either. That's why I have the bar. My therapist told me that I needed to get better at socializing. I'm not any better after four years." It was he who asked her if she'd had a lot of therapy. "More than most. I've had a—I guess you could call it a tragic life. Not only have I had a lot of death and mayhem in my life, but it's something that I don't share either."

"Toby saw her parents killed. Her grannie, too." She looked at Gracie when she spoke. "You're not a terrible person, Toby. But they should know that there is a reason for you being the way that you are. I promise you that no one here will judge you."

"Perhaps not, Gracie, but it was my story to tell if I wanted it." When she stood up, so did Gracie. Sebastian did as well. "What are you going to do? Hurt me?"

"No. I think that you've been hurt more than anyone I know. No, I don't want to hurt you, but I do believe that you need a good friend." She said she wasn't good with people. "You used to be. You used to be as lively as anyone that we knew. Then, you witnessed horrific murders, and it changed you. Come back to me."

"I can't." She turned to leave, and he stepped in front of her. He had no idea what possessed him to do that. He'd seen her in action before. "What do you want?"

"My name is Sebastian Gerald. I, too, have witnessed things that haunt me. My wife and my child were murdered one night. I survived so that I could testify against the men who had done it to them. When

I woke up from my coma, my life was forever changed. My wife and daughter had been gone and buried for two years by then. My grandma suffered for a month before someone helped her along by going back to the hospital and murdering her, too. I testified against Parker Roman. The boss mobster that wanted me to work for him, and I turned him down."

"He is still out there. You were put in protective custody, given a new name, an identity that they found out about." He nodded at her. "You disappeared. That's why Dick was trying to find you. He knew that you were on your way here. They won't stop, you know this, right?"

"I do. But when I heard from Wilhelm that my brother was looking for me, I told myself that this was a good way to end all of this. This hiding out. Not doing anything that I want to do. Like being with my little sister." She told him, not asked, that he'd changed his mind. "I have. I don't know why that only after a few hours, I've felt better than I have in a very long time. It's a feeling that I'm sure you're unfamiliar with, as I was. But being here, being with this family gives me more hope than I've had in a good long time."

"I'm happy for you, but what does that have to do with me?" Before he could tell her, she sat down in the chair that she'd just vacated. "They'll come for me now that I've killed one…his name was Roman as well, I'm betting. I'm a dead man."

"We both are." She sat in the chair for several minutes. The others had left them there, and he was glad for it. Sebastian had already told them more than he'd wanted. It had taken nothing for him to share it, either. "I'll help you against them. I've learned a few things myself since I've been out of the hospital."

"I'm a green beret. Special forces, as well as a part-time marshal. I've learned from the best." He nodded, knowing on some level that he didn't get all the information that she'd been trained to do. "What makes you think that I want to live any more than you did before coming here."

"I can see it in your face that you've had enough." She glared at him. "I've got a sister, remember? That doesn't hurt me."

"I don't want to…" She stood up, and he did again. "I'm going home. I think you have enough to deal with without me being here. I can almost feel the questions that they have for you."

"Don't. Please don't leave yet." She headed to the door. "Please, Toby. I've nothing to say to you to hold you here, but I will tell you that I've never felt so helpless until I met you. I feel that. I know that you're not going to like this, but I feel better with you around.

Like you could be my rock when I need it."

"I don't want to be anyone's rock, Sebastian. I have enough shit going on right now to fill up several needy bags." He laughed. Sebastian hadn't had a reason to laugh in a very long time. "You think I'm funny that I have baggage?"

"No. I don't think you're funny at all. But I do think it's funny how you described it. Needy bags? I like that." He put his hands up to hold her, but she took a step back. "I think I should have remembered that from last night. But I'm asking you, as a desperate man in a house full of people who want to help me, to please help me by staying."

She looked at the door and then back at him. Toby didn't say anything, but she was thinking. Not that he'd ever play poker or any other game of chance with her, but he knew that she was weighing her options. When she told him that she didn't want to be his friend, a little part of him hurt. But he nodded.

"I have a home near here. Do you think that we could go there for a little while? I need to chill out. To hit the bag." He asked her if that was going to be him. "No, dumbass, a punching bag. It's been a hard day for me. You too, I guess, but I'm not concerned about your pity party right now."

After telling Caleb that they'd be back—at least

he hoped so—the two of them got into the limo and headed back to her home. Christ, he thought when they pulled into the beautifully maintained drive, she really did have some money.

True to her word, she went upstairs to change. When she returned, with him a pair of trainers and a shirt, she made her way to the basement. The entire room that they entered was filled with the kind of equipment that would keep anyone in shape. Toby went to the heavy bag and began working it. Once he was changed into the too-large pants, he sat down at a state-of-the-art rowing machine. Hell, he thought, he'd live here with her if only he could use her gym. It was better than anything he'd ever used in most places before.

Rowing relaxed him. He also built up a good sweat. When he'd rowed about as much as he could, he went to the treadmill. Sebastian noticed that Toby was now on the rowing machine, and he was happy that he remembered to wipe it down when he was finished. After about two hours, she told him she was going to take a shower and that he was fine to join her.

"Is there any kind of sensor from your head to your mouth? I mean, you just asked me to join you in a shower." She told him that if he tried anything, she knew how to take care of herself. "Of that, I have no doubt."

He did join her in the shower and found that there was nothing sexual about it. He saw her scars; there were plenty of them, and she saw his. There weren't as many on his body, but hers were hatchet marks and other sharp-bladed marks, while his were bullet holes. When they were finished up, she asked him to lunch.

They were getting along fine, he thought, but they weren't talking about anything serious. He doubted that they would either. When lunch was finished. The two of them got dressed again and headed back to Calebs. He felt so much better about dealing with all of them—he was used to being alone than he had before. Sebastian would have to remember that. To hit the gym when he was feeling overwhelmed again. It had worked wonders on his mind and body.

Chapter 1

Sebastian slept better that night than he had in ages. He supposed it had a lot to do with the workout he'd had yesterday, but he didn't think that was entirely it. The family, his new family, had welcomed him into their home and hearts. Something so calming about them at times had him thinking that he'd been smart for coming here. But, as usual in his life, time would tell.

Toby Hayden had been a breath of fresh air for him. Also, she'd been the one who had taken him to her gym to work out. It was a way that she dealt with stress on her own, and he liked it. And her.

She was brash, harsh, and she didn't give a fuck who liked her or not. In fact, she told him that she didn't want to be his friend. Just like that, too, she didn't want to be anything to him. However much it hurt, he was glad that she didn't just give him what he wanted. It might well save their lives when it came time. Being friends with Caleb and the others was going to be scary enough, with the mob boss, Parker Roman, coming after him.

There was no doubt that they were in for trouble. Sebastian had had his entire family murdered, his child and wife, when he'd turned down the opportunity to work for Parker as a hitman for him. He's been a marksman in the service and was good at taking out a target when it came to that. However, working for a crook, no matter how much he put pressure on him to do so, he didn't think that he'd be able to live with himself if he took the job. There was enough death and murder going on without him adding to the count.

Toby had come into his life just when he had arrived at his brother's town. She'd actually inadvertently killed a man who came into her bar looking for him. He didn't think that he'd ever forget the way she just pulled out a hatchet and took his arm off. But Caleb had welcomed him, as had all the family into his home. However, he wasn't sure how welcoming they'd be if Parker found out where he was. But Caleb and the others assured him that he was in good hands. He had a feeling that they didn't understand what sort of person that Parker was. He hoped that they'd never find out, but after the incident at the bar that Toby owned, he was thinking that they were a bit closer than he'd thought.

The man Richard Roman, brother to Parker, had come into her bar the night before last and demanded that she tell him where the Anderson person was that was looking for his brother. He'd had a firsthand view of what she'd been able to do in order to kill the man. While she knew Harlin and some about Caleb from living around town all her life, she didn't tell him anything. When he grabbed her, demanding that she stop lying to him, she ended up killing the man because he didn't take no for an answer. Sebastian couldn't believe that men now days didn't listen when they were told no. Toby was good at protecting herself, and it made him smile every time he thought of the man being killed by a slip of a girl. But she was far from that.

Looking around the room that he'd been assigned, or he supposed given was a nicer way to say it, he realized that he wasn't keen on it. It was beautifully decorated. The bed was soft, and there were little touches around the room that reminded him of the couple that lived here. Especially Tabby. In fact, he could see that she'd had a hand in decorating all of the house without the benefit of decorators. It was homey. Clean and comfy. Old and new. It was just not for him.

Getting up, he made his way downstairs. After asking about dinner plans from the cook, he was told that Caleb and Tabby both had said that they'd be home by six. He made a decision right then that he was going to dine alone. Let them dine alone, too. Telling the cook that he'd be getting something in town, he made his way outside. It was, he just realized, a beautiful little town.

Sebastian wandered around the town for several hours. He'd found the library as well as the bank. Getting himself an account, using one of the many aliases that he'd had made for himself, he opened not just a checking account but also got himself a safety deposit box to store his cash in. It startled him every time he looked in his backpack how much money his grannie had left him when she'd passed away.

After his mom dropped him off one day and never returned for him, he lived out his childhood with his mother's mom. She was a mean old woman, bitter about a lot of things, but she truly loved him. And he had her. While he was younger, she taught him all kinds of survival tactics. Then, when it was obvious that she wasn't going to be around much longer, just after he got out of the service, he went to stay with her again.

"I've been putting cash all over the house for

you to take and go. The land, all fifty thousand acres, is in your name now, too. As soon as I go into hospice, I want you to sell it off to the highest bidder. Then, before my body is even cold, you light out of here. Them kids of mine will want a piece of it, and I don't want you to share with them at all. I want you to have it all. If'n you don't leave before they pounce on this town, my damned kids will wonder where all their inheritance is, and they'll hunt you down. But I taught you how to avoid them. You keep yourself away from them, and you'll be a happy man." He had asked her about her funeral. "You don't need to be hanging around to see me all dolled up in no coffin, Sebastian. You and I have had the best years that we can, and I couldn't love you any more than I do. You go on, or they'll hurt you. And they'll steal from you until all my hard work is for nothing. You hear me?"

So he did what she wanted. The morning that they came to get her, to take her for her final days, he'd sold off all the land for a substantial amount of money, gathered up the cash that she'd listed for him to find, and then took to the streets. Walking from Colorado to Ohio had given him a great perspective of the country, and he wouldn't have done it any differently if he'd had to do it over again. Now that he was here, he felt just a little that he could relax. But not too much. Not only was the mob after him but his deadbeat family as well.

He found himself on the street that Toby lived on just after lunch. There were houses on the street that were as big as hers was but not nearly as well maintained. The mansion, no other word for it, gleamed with old wealth. The yard and the landscaping were well maintained, and the oversized eight-car garage just to the right of the house looked like it had been there forever. However, Toby had told him that her father had had it built just before he'd been killed to house his extensive old car collection. He hadn't lived long enough to see it finished.

Walking up to the front door, he wasn't positive that he'd be welcomed. He couldn't for the life of him understand why he'd come here in the first place. When he rang the doorbell, the door opened with a man dressed in all gray. It made him want to laugh just a little when he heard Toby behind him fussing at the man.

"I told you that I had it. Herman, I swear to you, you listen to me less and less as you get older." Toby looked at him and then asked him what he wanted. Before he could answer her, even if he'd been able to think of a good reason to be there, she invited him in. "I was just going to have some lunch. I don't know what we're having, but you're more than welcome to join me. Let's not make a habit of just showing up. Call next time."

"All right. I don't know why I'm here." She seemed to understand and nodded. "Thanks for inviting me in. I don't know what I would have done – I guess I just would have gone back to Caleb's and stayed in my room. I feel like an outsider in their home."

"I know that feeling." Entering the kitchen, the room smelled like his grandma's home. Cinnamon and sugar. The smell of fried potatoes cooked with bacon grease. There was a large pitcher of brown liquid on the work table that he'd bet anything was filled with tea. The cook, he couldn't remember her name, was just pulling another plate from the cabinet when he was asked to be seated. The three of them, including the butler, were going to have lunch together. "This is my cook and friend, Ginger Marshall. She and her husband run the house for me. This is Herman, butler, driver, and whatever else I need for him to do."

"Good to meet you." Whatever he expected out of having lunch with them, it wasn't at all what they had. It was like they had decided to put tabs with what they had around written onto the papers and put them into a large hat and pulled out things to have. He thought that it was the best meal he'd ever had since his grandma had gotten too weak to cook for the two of them anymore.

There were fried potatoes, and the drink was unsweetened iced tea. Cinnamon rolls, along with a bowl of fruit for each of them. The sandwiches, something that Ginger told him, were open-faced sandwiches, roasted chicken in a thick gravy poured over a thick slice of bread with mashed potatoes. Lots of carbs, really, but he wasn't going to complain. It was filling and homey. He couldn't have liked it any better because of the company.

After lunch and loaded down with carbs, Toby invited him out on the deck. Following her, he stood in the doorway to the 'deck' and marveled at what greeted him. Christ, to call it a simple deck was understating things. It was a place right out of a magazine. It was simply beautiful.

"My grannie loved the outdoors. Year round. So when she and grandda came to live with us, my dad had this put in for her. The large screens will be covered up in the winter months with glass panels, and the heat will be turned on. Though we don't use it much, the heat, I mean, the sunroof makes it nice and cozy out here. Also, this serves as a place to eat when the pool is open. I've not bothered with it this year as it's just me, but I think that was a mistake. I missed being able to come out here for a midnight swim." He asked her about her grandda. "I'm going to go and see him today. You should come. He just answers questions with a nod or shake of his head. He does tell me that he should have protected grandma better. I don't know how he would have done that. He'd been the first person that had been hurt and nearly died from the injuries."

"I'm not going to pry, but you were hurt that day as well, I'm guessing. The hatchet marks on you show that you were hurt badly, too, right?" She didn't look like she was going to answer, but she finally nodded. "How long ago was this? I'm assuming that it's been at least a few years."

"Twenty. I was seven. My brother was five. Mom and dad were just about to celebrate their tenth anniversary the next night. The house, more than likely how the man got in, was being overrun by caterers as well as decorators. The back yard was decorated as well as most of the house, by that last night. The finishing touches were supposed to be done the next morning. The guy, David Rochester, hid in the basement until it was just us at home." She looked at him. "I'm about to tell you the part that I've never told anyone else. Not even my therapist. But David was young, twenty as a matter of fact. However, everyone knew that, but he was slightly mentally handicapped. He wanted my dad to hire him so that he could get a paycheck. He told him that he'd even be willing to not go into work every day so that he'd not be pressed into doing something that he didn't know how to do. David told my dad, while he was standing in the living room covered in blood, that he just wanted a paycheck so that he could prove to his dad that he wasn't a deadbeat. He'd already hit grandda and nearly killed him. Thomas, my little brother, was dead or dying by then. David removed his head with a hatchet in one move. Once he killed my grandma, my grandda dying on the floor, dad told him that he'd hire him, just to let his wife and child go. David must have realized that it wasn't going to work at some point, and he raped and killed my mother. Then he started on me."

"I'm so sorry, Toby. I can't imagine what your father might have gone through to see his parents and children killed." She thanked him. "What else happened? There is more, I'm assuming."

"Dad attacked him when he got close enough for him to do so. I don't know how he'd done it, but Dad had been able to get out of the rope that he'd been tied with. My dad was no pushover, so he was able to get in a few well-placed blows to David as well. He died from the wounds, I was told. But when he hit my dad with the hatchet in the head, it was sticking out of his skull. Before he could, if that was his plan to finish off me, the police had arrived. Grandda had crawled, with his insides hanging out of him, to his cell phone and called the police. I think that was the only thing that saved the two of us."

"You said that your grandda was in a nursing home." She told him that he'd given up on the world and wanted to die. "Sounds to me like he's the hero in all this. Does he know that? Poor man."

"I tell him that all the time. However, since I seem to feel the same way that he does about life, he doesn't want to hang out with me anymore." Sebastian laughed. "You find this funny?"

"No. Not what happened. Never that. But just thinking about the two of you hanging out. I have a feeling that he and you are like two peas in a pod, as my grannie was so fond of saying." She smiled and told him that they were forever plotting something or another that would get them both in trouble when she was younger. "I can see that. Though I've never met him, I'm betting that he's a pistol and speaks his mind just as much as you do."

"Now, that would be wrong. I never spoke my mind until this happened with my family. It sort of brought me out—I was such a girly girl when I was younger. Would get upset with a single spot of dirt on my little dresses. Wouldn't dare leave the house with my mom unless I was dressed well with my hair done up. Then, after this, I just found it useless to even put forth the effort for much in wanting to impress. I've gotten better over the years, but I don't have it in me to try and make an impression on anyone." She looked at him. "Which makes me wonder why you're seeking me out. You do understand that I'm not fit for company. That I can barely make myself go to work when I have to. I'm a mess."

"I don't know why either. But there is something so calming about you that I feel better myself with you around." He laid his head back on the chair he was in and closed his eyes. "I've not had a moment's reprieve since I was about fourteen, and my mother tired to kidnap me from my grannie and shot me up full of drugs so that I'd not run away. I'd had a good life until then. But after that, it was a serious shit going on that I couldn't get a grasp on anymore."

~*~

Donald was nervous. He'd not had a lot to do with his brother and sisters since their momma had died, and they'd all been put in jail for attacking the limo that she'd been riding in. He'd gotten to go and see her before they burned her up, thanks to Ms. Tabby. It hurt him still that he'd been such a bad boy to her all these years. While he was sure that she understood that it was all William's fault—to not act like he did would get him beaten to snot, not that he still should have done it—but he missed her.

"All Rise for the Honorable Lance Coldwell, the presiding judge in the state of Ohio, town of Dresden." Donald stood up immediately, but he watched the other three, his brother and sisters, as they fought and argued about who was going to stand up first. He didn't understand why William, as the oldest, thought that everything should revolve around him. Actually, Donald had been thinking about a lot of things that had to do with his brother. Almost as soon as they were up, they were told to have a seat again. Donald sat still, hoping that none of his family would realize that he wasn't sitting with them. But almost as soon as he tried to make himself look small, his brother found him.

"What are you doing way over there, Donald James? Get your ass over here with the rest of us. I done told you that we're going to be tried together. I don't care what you have some fancy pants telling you. We're family, and since I'm the oldest, I say what goes. My way, they'll have to split up our time four ways and not three. Get your butt over here like I said." He told him, for the first time in his life, that he was just fine on his own. "Perhaps you didn't hear me right. I said to get your butt over here and—where did all your fat go? What have they been doing to you, Donald James? Holding out on your meals so you'd be skinny? I'll take care of this for you. See that I don't."

"I don't want you to take care of anything, William. I'm fine right here. I decided—yeah, *I* decided that I was going to be on my own in here. I don't cotton to you telling me what to do no more. I got me a good attorney too in Mr. Palmer here." Mr. Palmer told him that he didn't have to talk to them if he didn't want to. "Hear that, William? I don't have to talk to you if I don't want to. Now, you leave me be."

When William started to stand up, caught up in his chains, he fell on his butt. Donald knew better than to laugh at his older brother, but it sure was funny watching him wrestle around, trying to get up off the floor again. It took four men and a chair to get him up again. Then he glared at him like it was his fault. Donald was getting mighty sick of being treated like everything going on was his fault. He'd seen the light, so to speak, he thought.

His attorney told him that he could maybe get out in a year, no more than five. He'd been cooperating with the police people about things that William had done, too. Also, his sisters. Betsy Sue wasn't so bad as

April Showers, but she was mean as a rattle snake when things didn't go her way. Which he'd come to realize was a lot. He sort of listened in while the judge was telling his family that he had decided to go separate from them and that his trial was next. Not that he was a good man, either. He'd been led around by his brother since he was old enough to walk. But no more. He was standing up for himself even if he got the snot beat out of him again. Donald looked at the paperwork that was in front of him.

Donald couldn't read a lick of it. There were a few letters that he was beginning to know, like the first three. But they didn't do him any good when they were all jumbled up with the rest of them. Mr. Palmer handed him a pencil and paper to play with. He'd been a durn site better to him than his family had been in all his life, with the exception of Ms. Tabby and his grannie.

Donald wasn't smart. He knew that he had a low IQ. He couldn't read, write, or even add stuff up. While he did know his numbers to say them, usually, he would get them messed up in order and have to start all over again. But that was all right, Mr. Palmer told him. That was what was going to get him out of prison.

When he realized that something was going on

in the room, he looked at where his family was sitting. William was making a fuss again about something, and April Showers wasn't having any of it. He'd heard tell that both his sisters were divorced now. Not that he could find fault with their husbands wanting nothing to do with them. But since his wife, Lisa, had left him too, he thought it was sad. And lonely. But he did have him a friend in the police station who was helping him out with stuff. She even made sure that he had some fitting clothing for today, too.

"Mr. Donald Pastor, what do you have to say to the accusations that your brother is making against you?" He didn't know because he'd not been paying attention but only had to look at his attorney for him to answer. He said that William had been leading Donald down a path of mayhem and destruction since he'd been a child and didn't know any better. "I have all the paperwork there on the testing that you have had done, Mr. Palmer. I thank you for that."

Tuning out again, he continued to draw on his paper and think about the things that William had done in the name of getting money from their momma. Or anybody, for that matter. Donald had never once hit her, not where it would hurt her anyway. Momma had been so good to him, the only person in the world he thought that had been. As he thought about all the times that he and his momma would get together, it hurt him deeper in the heart. Donald sure did miss his momma.

When he was poked, gentle like by Mr. Palmer, he stood up when asked. William and the others were being dragged out, and he was standing there alone. Mr. Palmer told him to tell the judge what he'd been thinking about the day that his brother had killed the limo driver.

"We was in the car, yes sir. We had to go along with what William wanted, or he'd beat us up. Especially me. He said that I was too stupid to argue about how bad it was going to be, so I was just to do as he told me. I didn't know he was going to keep doing it. Hitting that car. Then, when it was rolled over on its top part, he started yelling at us to go there and drag momma out so that he could take care of Blackbird." He asked him who that was. "Oh, Ms. Raven. She's a good person, that one is. When I asked to talk to her about me not being with my family in this here courtroom today, she got a hold of Mr. Palmer here lickety-split, and he's been real nice to me. I been talking to the police too about stuff. Did they tell you that?"

"Yes, they did. So you want to make a change in your life, do you?" He didn't understand, so he looked at Mr. Palmer. When he nodded, Donald, in turn, nodded to the judge. "Good for you. Also, I'm not sure if you were made aware of this or not, but the autopsy showed that your mother died from injuries that she sustained in the accident that day. Two counts of vehicular homicide carries a hefty prison sentence. Were you driving the car that day, Mr. Donald?"

"No, sir. I don't know nothing about driving. William was." He glanced down at his paper and then back at the judge, just a little confused. "My momma didn't die that day, sir. She was burned up after she died, having a good time with the kiddies. I don't know where you heard your information, but that's what they told me."

"What I mean is, sir, and I'm sorry you weren't informed until today, but your momma had a blood clot that she got when she was in that car accident. It was a tiny little thing they found later, but it was what killed her that day." He asked him if William hitting the car over and over was what gave her the clod. "Blood clot, but yes, that's what the coroner is ruling. That she was murdered by the car being in an accident."

"William killed our momma? He went, and…we told him not to do it. All of us did. But he hit Besty Sue when she said she wanted out. So, we had to pretend to be on his side. He's powerful mean—he went and killed our momma?" He sat down then, lying his head on the table. Sobbing as quietly as he could so as he'd not be called names, Donald hurt badder than he did before. Just knowing that his momma was having a good time when she passed was all right, but this here? William killing her off. It was more than he could take.

Mr. Palmer handed him a box of tissues but didn't tell him to get over it like William would have. He told him how sorry he was that she'd been killed and that it was just one more thing to blame on his older brother. Nodding when he could, Donald stood up and looked at the judge. He didn't make fun of him either.

"I'm profoundly sorry for your loss, Donald. I know she's been gone for over a couple of months now, but it still hurts. Finding out that she could still be around, well, I can't imagine what you must be feeling toward your brother for his part in her early demise." Donald wasn't positive about what demise meant, but he thought it had to do with her dying. "Now. Let me tell you what I've done today with the other three. I've separated their trials. Like you, I think your sisters have been doing what William wanted for years, and it's ingrained in them to follow along. I'm charging William with two counts of homicide along with the things that you've been able to help the police with. Also, your sisters and you have a few to answer to as well. But I'm not concerned with the petty stuff at the moment. If I were to reduce your sentence, Donald, to say two years, what would you do with your life? I need a good answer and one that you're going to do too."

"Well, sir. I've been thinking on that a lot. Mr. Palmer told me that I might get me some time off for helping. He didn't promise, but he did tell me to think on it. I want to go away. Move away and never see them again. I did have me a thinking on my sisters, but they'd be hard to be around all the time and not get us in trouble." The judge thought that was about right. "I want to get me a job. My first one ever, and make me some money on my own. I don't want to—stealing don't help you at all, they told me in them classes I've been taking at the jail. It has…" He looked at Mr. Palmer, who told him what it did. "That's right. The tickle-down effect. Where if'n I steal from someone, they don't have no food for their kids. Then the kids don't have a good meal, they don't study very hard." Mr. Palmer corrected him. "Oh. Trickle-down effect. Not tickle."

"It seems to me that you're making good use of your time in jail, Donald. I'm glad to hear that." He thanked him and told him that he'd been collecting rocks, too. "Rocks?"

"Yes, sir. I was just sitting around on my bottom when I got my free time. I was told that walking would let me find all kinds of things." He moved up to the big shelf that the judge was on and handed him a rock. "Mr. Palmer's granddaughter, she has one of them polishing machines, and she shined this right up for me. After I seen what I could do with them pretty rocks, I started walking more and more. I lost me about seventy pounds, they say. And I feel good. You can have that one. It's my favorite, but I want you to have it."

"I wish I could, Donald, but it might be taken the wrong way if I take this from you. It is a lovely rock, however." He put it back in his pocket and went back to his table. "All right, Donald. You let them bring you back here tomorrow, and you and I will have a conversation with Mr. Palmer, all right?"

"Yes, sir. I don't mind going back to the jail none. They moved me away from the others, and I been sleeping like a baby. Also, it's real nice to have a soft bed that my brother doesn't take from me on account of him wanting it more. Thank you for that." As he was being taken back to the jail, Donald felt good. He was going to make his momma proud of him while she was up in heaven, and when he saw her, he was going to have only good things to tell her about his life.

Chapter 2

Heather looked over the paperwork that she'd been given and couldn't make heads or tails out of it. Hiring a detective to find Sebastian had been costly, but without someone telling her what he'd found, it wasn't doing her a bit of good. She handed it off to her brother, Roger. He laid it on the table and ignored her for the phone call he was on.

"Yes, I'm aware that the will has been read and that it was finalized, but there wasn't anything there for us to take. Not even the land nor—how the hell did she have so much land and not telling us about it? Or, for that matter, who said that Sebastian could sell it off without our permission?" The man must have answered him because Roger rolled his eyes. "I don't care what you say about my mother. There isn't any way that she was of sound mind when she wrote out that will. Where the hell does she get off, leaving us nothing at all when we were her blood relatives?" Roger laid his phone on the table and put it on speaker so she could hear the attorney that their mom had hired.

"Mr. Gerald, I know for a fact that I handed you the paperwork that your mother had filled out about how much you and your sister and brother owed her. Several hundred thousand dollars each was either stolen or borrowed from her over the years. You said that you understood it." He said that was before they found out that there wasn't anything for them. "Be that as it may, your mother kept meticulous records of her transactions with you and the other two, and she says that there wasn't any way that she was going to leave any of you anything since you more than made up for any goodwill that she had for you when you were children. She thought that the three of you would flitter it away, and there would be nothing left of it for her grandchild."

"You mean Sebastian Gerald? My sister's kid?" He said that was right. "So on account of Heather leaving her brat with mom all these years, we all get nothing. That's not the least bit fair if you ask me. My brother and I have plans for that money. I want you to hunt Sebastian down and have him divide it like it should have been in the first place. If his mother wants to share with him, then that's fine. I don't, so he needs to give me my third. Or better yet, half of it to me since I've had to waste all my time in doing this crap to get the money that I'm owed in the first place."

"Owed, Mr. Gerald? What about the money that the three of you owed her? I'm sure that she would like to have known that you were really going to pay her back?" He told the man that it was water under the bridge as his mom was dead and that he was still alive. The money would do her no good now. "Well, it won't do you any good either, as she didn't feel it necessary to leave it to you three. Please do not call my office again. You will not be put through to any of the offices here, so don't bother wasting your time. I've read the will, and that was all my part was about when she passed away. She was a good grandma to that boy, and you should just leave him alone."

When the line went dead, she glared at her brother. "What the hell do you mean I can share with my son? I no more wanted him than I did not being able to party all the time. And you certainly aren't getting half. Do you expect that Conner and I share the other half? No, that's not how it works. We each get a third." She thought of something. "You either take a third, Roger, or I'll have my son not share with you at all." Her brother laughed.

"You think that he's going to come running to you when you want him to? That your darling little boy is going to have a thing to do with you after the way that you treated him when he was a teenager?" He laughed harder. "You'll be lucky if he doesn't haul off and hit you, Heather, after the shit that you did to him. From what I heard, it took him a full month of monitoring to make sure that he didn't die from the drugs you fed him. Not to mention the beatings that you hired guys to do to him. Why on earth do you think he'd have a thing to do with you now?"

"Because I'm his mother, dumbass." He pointed out that their mother had left them high and dry, too. "She was a bitch. And she never wanted us in the first place."

"Oh, I don't know about that. She did want us. And she was a good mom to all three of us. Right up until we weren't to her. I'm not saying that I would have changed the way that I treated her when we got out of the house, but we gave her no reason to keep on loving us when we were gone. Not that it makes what she did to us any better, but I'm just saying she did want us around at one time. I think that you and Conner were the worst to her. Leaving her broke like you did. At least I didn't take all her money and run."

"No, just most of it. Did you ever find out how

much was made off the land? I'm sure that it wasn't a small amount." He asked her if she knew that Mom had owned thirty thousand acres of land. "No. That's not possible. If she would have owned that, don't you think she would have given some of it to us before she died?"

"Absolutely not. By the time we could have used the land, she was already set on keeping it away from us." He looked at the paperwork but didn't pick it up. "Thirty thousand acres of land just sitting there for us to sell off, and we didn't have a clue. Your son sold it before she was gone. It was in his name long before he got out of the service, too. We might could have fooled Mom, but not him. He was always too sharp for us getting around Mom and would keep it from us better—if he'd just allowed us in the house once in a while, we could have figured a few things out and made some hard cash. But no, he had to stand there at the door with a gun pointed at us. Then, even when he wasn't there? Christ, when I think of that fucking bastard shooting my car up just because I was 'trespassing.' Little fucker. When I see him, he's going to pay for that."

Heather knew that she couldn't take any credit for Sebastian being smart. She'd had nothing to do with his upbringing. But she did, just a little to herself, let herself believe that she'd been the one teaching him how to swindle his uncles. But why her? She was going to ask him when she saw him. A son and their mom were supposed to be close, right? She asked herself.

Finally, Roger picked up the paperwork from the investigator. She went to the kitchen to get herself another beer and offered one to Roger. Heather knew that he'd not take it. Beer was just too low-brow for him. Conner, who'd been sleeping on the couch in the living room, perked up when she snapped the lid off of her own drink.

"Bring me one of them, Heather. I got me a powerful thirst for that." He always had a powerful thirst when it was someone else's beer. When he drank it straight down, he reached for hers, and she moved out of his reach. "Oh, come on, sis. I told you I was thirsty."

"When you buy the next case, then you can get your fill. This is my place and my beer." It really wasn't her place, and they all knew it. She was living off the government's dime. Heather didn't know what they'd do if they ever found out that she didn't have Daisy, the baby that she no longer knew where she was, with her all this time. She'd been telling them that she'd been with her daddy when they came around to see her. Like she even knew who her daddy was.

The knock at the door startled her. Going to the door after putting her beer in the cabinet, she opened it to see the police standing there. Before she could get her wits about her and figure out what they wanted, she was shoved a blue file in her chest and knocked back a few steps.

"Ms. Gerald, we're here to inspect your home." She said that they couldn't do that without notice. The man only opened her mailbox on the door and handed her about a week's worth of mail. "It was mailed out to you two weeks ago with this date on it. You signed for it, and the man who had delivered it said that you were either drunk or hungover and put it in your mail slot. You signed for it."

They went through her home like they owned the place. Tearing up the living room where Conner was sitting without a care that he was there. Once they made it to the bedrooms, she knew she was going to be out on her ass soon. She'd been using the extra bedrooms for growing pot for the last four years. It helped her with money when she needed it.

"Well, well, well. What do we have here?" She told them that she'd never seen that room before, and that went over badly. The inspector had her put in cuffs, as well as her brothers, as they were there with her. Christ, this wasn't going at all like she had planned.

"I have a message for you, Ms. Gerald. The woman who turned you in said that if you three were to stop looking for Sebastian, she'd help you out. Otherwise, we're to prosecute you to the max."

"Who would turn me in around here? Nobody, that's who. And what does this woman mean about not looking for my son? He's my fucking son." He asked her where her daughter was. "She's visiting her father."

"We've contacted him before coming here. At least the name on her birth certificate was who we contacted. He said that Daisy could have been conceived by any number of men that you've shared your bed with. That he'd not be taking any kind of trouble associated with you until you proved beyond a shadow of a doubt that she was indeed his daughter. And she's not. We tested him while we were talking to him." She asked them why they'd do that. "Because, Ms. Gerald, you've been collecting government benefits since she was born. We have also heard — with proof that she hasn't lived with you since she was two years old. You've been lying to the government offices for years, and it's finally, I'm happy to say, caught up with you."

Roger was laughing as he was taken out to the cruiser. Conner was cursing, and he was good at it, when he was put into a separate cruiser than either one of them. Heather didn't know what this was all about, but she was handed a cell phone, a really nice one, as soon as she was put in the back seat. She thanked the man for it.

"It's not for you. There is a person on the other end who wishes to speak to you. Then you're to give me the phone back." Heather said he'd have to take it from her. "Don't think that I won't either. Talk to her." After saying hello, she had to wait on the person. It did sound like a woman to stop laughing before she would speak to her.

"Heather Lynne Gerald?" She said that was her name. "I have been doing a bit of research on you. Seems to me that you're not nearly as nice as you think you are."

"So? What the fuck do you want? I'm sort of in the middle of something here." She told her to hang on. "I don't have time to hang on. I've been arrested for something I didn't do."

"Hello, mother." Heather felt like her entire mind just emptied in that moment. "It's Sebastian in the event you didn't know my voice. Though I don't know why you would. I've not spoken to you in decades. I will tell you that Daisy is safe from you and anyone else you might be trying to send after us. And I'd not expect to hear from her anytime soon. Also, you and your brothers aren't going to be getting any of Grannie's money either."

"Why not? Christ, Sebastian, I'm your mother for fucks sake. The very least you can do is to—"

"The very least that I can do is to ignore you as you have done to me. And I will. As soon as this call is over with, I'm finished with the three of you." She asked him why he'd bother her then. "You talk to the other two into dropping this pursuit of me, or I'll go to the police on some of the other shit that I've found on you and my uncles. You'll think that bilking the government was easy street before I'm finished with you."

"You don't have shit. Besides, who would believe you anyway? You've stolen our inheritance and ran off with my child. Where is she, Sebastian? I'm sure that the courts will believe me over you. I've had a lot of practice about making myself out to be the poor little woman scorned by her only son." He laughed. She might have thought it was a good laugh, but she didn't want to give him anything that would make it sound like she was happy with him. "So you find it funny that I'm going to run you through? That I'm going to get all the money, and you'll have shit?"

"No. I think it's funny that you really believe that you could fool anyone after the shit that I've found out about you. Especially about how you got Daisy." She felt her face go pale. Dread like nothing she'd ever felt rolled over her. "Ah, I can tell by your silence that you know what I'm talking about. It wasn't bad enough that you took their child from them when they'd only just had her, but to kill them both in a fit of what I can only assume was rage, too, is something I think that the police will be happy to hear about."

"You wouldn't." Not only did he laugh again, but he told her that he was going to tell on her anyway. "Why? What harm did I do to those people? They couldn't afford her anyway. And I needed proof that I had a kid since you wouldn't cooperate with me."

"You drugged me, and then when you weren't getting the things you wanted, you drove by the emergency department and tossed me out of the door while still moving." She smiled at that memory. "Grannie also knew some of the things that the three of you got up to once you left home. Shall I list a few of them for you? I will here in a second. I want you to tell your brothers to back off. Or else. I'm not fucking around with you anymore, mother. Do it or don't, I don't care, but I will ruin the three of you if you don't. In fact, I probably will anyway. I don't trust your word any more than I do a lot of things that you've told me over the years."

"You think you know so much, do you? Well, have at it, son. Tell me what sort of juicy information you have that will get your mother into trouble. I don't believe you have shit just so you know." He told her about the three children that she'd helped kidnap and sell with a friend of hers. "Yeah? Prove it. There is nothing you can say that makes me think you know much about that."

"All right. You want good stuff. How about the fact that you and your brothers killed your father. That you lured him out to the barn one evening because you told him that you saw someone in the barn. Then, when he was out there, each of you took an axe and hit him several times with them. After he was dead, the three of you went to the creek and washed up, leaving your bloodied clothing to run downstream so that it wouldn't be in the house." She laid her head back and wondered at how he'd gotten so much information. "Then there is the time that Conner raped a young woman, nearly killing her. Not that it mattered that he didn't kill her then. You and Roger snuck her body into the trash dump and cut her up, feeding her body to the animals there so that you wouldn't be caught. Want more? I have it."

She had no doubt that he did, too. Just the couple of things that he'd mentioned, she thought for sure

they'd gotten away with. Christ, love a duck. She was
going to be in deep shit if she couldn't convince her
little boy — a man now, she supposed that she wanted
him in her life and that they could start over. Heather
was just working up to saying a few things to get in
on his tender side when the woman was back on the
phone.

"You leave him alone, do you hear me, Heather?
I have a great deal of money, and I'm not afraid to
spend it to get you and those two morons that you're
related to put away for good. By prison or grave, at this
point, I don't care." She asked her who she thought she
was. "The one that is going to be bringing you to heel
like the dog that — no, not dog. They're too kind and
loving to be associated with you. No, I'm just going to
make sure you pay for what you three have done."

When the line went silent, the phone was jerked
from her hands. She didn't even get to admire it for a
second; the cop snatched it from her so quickly. Asking
what his deal was, he turned in the seat and smiled at
her. It wasn't a friendly smile either.

"She said that I could have the phone after she
was finished with you. There might be another time
that she wants to speak to you." Heather wanted to
beg the man to allow her to go free. Showing a little tit
usually worked but not for this man. "Christ, put that

away before I get sick. When was the last time that you had a shower? Not to mention, change your bra? That thing is as dirty as your fucking skin."

Feeling about as low as she'd been in a long time, Heather sat in the back seat without saying a word to the two cops with her. She'd show them. Not talking to them, or in this case, she supposed it would be joining in on their conversation, was going to teach them that they couldn't talk to her like that and get away with it. Bastards. All men were bastards.

~*~

"I didn't know it would be that easy." Toby told him that with enough money, she was sure that anyone could find the most determined of creatures. "I suppose. That's what Caleb says, anyway. I've not used my money for evil just yet."

When she laughed, it brought a smile to his face. He'd been staying with her over the last few days, and he had never felt so good. There was plenty to occupy his mind in the form of books to read. There was also a computer that he could use in his room, she'd told him. At night, when she went to work, he'd go with her just to hang out with the others in the bar and with Toby. She was easy to get along with, and he thought that they had a good hamburger and fries meal that he could have eaten daily.

"What would you call this thing that we're doing?" He asked Toby what she meant. "You know, us living here. Not that I mind. I've not shared a residence with anyone but staff since...well, my family was killed. But I'm finding that I like having you around. You're not too gabby. You don't go on and on about one thing. And I feel safe with you here. Not that I couldn't take care of myself, but it's comforting to know that you're here with me. Does that make sense?"

"It does. Those are the very reasons that I like being here, too." He looked at her then. "Also, and I'm not being sexist or anything, but you're not hard on the eyes either. You're beautiful. Charming when you want to be and hard-assed when you don't. You don't prattle on either. Also, I just enjoy having you here if I have something to say. You know, like an old married couple."

"Do you want to be?" Again, he had to ask her what she meant. "Will you marry me? I'm jumping the gun here a little, but I don't want this to end. We don't have to be romantically or sexually involved or anything. Just like you said, two old people marrying so that they have each other."

"You don't love me." She shook her head and smiled at him. "I don't love you either. I like you. A great deal, but no, I don't love you. Not to say that I someday might fall in love with you, but that's not what we have now." She agreed with him.

"Sure. I'll marry you." He laid his head back on the chair he was reclining in. "So long as you know that when I do fall in love with you, Toby, it will be the forever kind of love. When I fall in love with you, too, I want us to be able to do what we're doing now, and nothing changes."

"I can agree to that. How about children? I know that at that point, we'll need to have sex. But for now, I was just wondering if children would be in our picture." He looked over at her before closing his eyes again. "I guess we don't have to have sex. I mean, adoption isn't out of the question. But just curious."

"I'd like some children. However, it's not my choice as to if we have them. I fully believe that it's your body and your decision to have them. Not that I wouldn't enjoy seeing you heavy with our child, but that's a long way off, don't you think?" She told him how old she was. "I'm thirty, so I think we have a bit of time, don't you?"

"I don't know. To be honest with you, before I asked you to marry me, I was going to see if you'd father a child with me. I want a baby of my own. Two or three, as a matter of fact. Little versions of you and me." When she laughed, he turned to her again. "I guess what I'm saying is that while I'd like to have you as my husband, I do. I would like to have some children right away."

Standing up, he put out his hand to her. If she took it, he was going to take her to the bedroom of her choice to make love to her in. He didn't know her schedule if she was ready to have a child or not, but he was willing to keep trying until they hit on the right time. She looked at his hand and then up at him.

"Would you mind calling your sister-in-law and having her file a marriage certificate for us? With your legal name? If we conceive today, I want to be able to tell our child that he or she was made while we were married. I know that it doesn't usually work out that way, getting knocked up on the first try, but I would like it." He asked her if she wanted him to sign anything, like a prenup. "You have money too, correct?"

"I do. Not as much as I think you do, but I have a few million." She nodded and then asked him if he wanted her to sign a prenup. "No. Like I suggested, you have a great deal more money than I do. It seems nuts to have you sign something that says you get what I willingly donate to this family. I'm assuming that you and I would be a family after this."

"Yes." She took his hand into her much smaller one and smiled up at him. "You don't act like you think that I'm insane. I mean, I proposed to you, offered you my body for procreation with only knowing each other for about a week. That's not nuts to you?"

"No. I don't...I didn't say this before, Toby, but I could easily fall in love with you. Hell, I've never been in love before, so I could very well be on the edge of it now. There is so much about you that I look forward to every day. Seeing you, talking to you. Even just being in the same room with you is enough for me to be around you. Adding children and romance just seems to me, anyway, like the icing on the cake. I believe that we'll be good for each other. Don't you?" She nodded and laid her head on his chest when she stood up. It was then that he realized what the bell sounding was. "Toby, your phone is ringing."

Toby had told him there were only three people who had the house phone number. The pizza place they ordered from, her attorney, and the nursing home. He had a feeling that it was the nursing home.

Going into the living room, then the great hall where she was standing, he took her hand when she put it out for him. As she talked to the person on the other end, he knew it was just as he thought. The home was calling about her grandfather. If that old man took today to die, he was going to be sorely disappointed in him. When she hung up the old-fashioned phone, she laid her head on his chest again. Holding her, he waited to see what he had to do to slay her dragons for her.

"That was the nursing home where my grandda is. He wants to see me. Now. I don't want to go. I'm terrified he's going to tell me he's finally had enough and that he is going to die. If he does that, today of all days, I'm going to beat him silly." Sebastian told her that he'd been thinking the same thing. Toby looked up at him. "Call your family. Tell them what we want, and we'll tell grandda that he is going to miss so much if he decides that he'd rather be dead than a great-grandfather. The old poop."

While he spoke to Caleb, telling him what he needed, he watched Toby stomp up the stairs to the second floor. Caleb was laughing so hard about something that he had to tell him to calm down twice before he could tell him the information that was needed to file their marriage certificate.

"I tell you what, Sebastian. You want to make the old man happy? There is a little guy at the hospital right now that has been abandoned. He's four months old. I have his name right here." He told Toby what was going on, and she seemed excited. He put it on speakerphone for her to hear, too. "His name is Kelly Tucker Garnett. His parents tried to raise him on their own, two kids themselves, and couldn't do it. Before they did something really stupid — it doesn't say what here, her mother told her to take him to the hospital or fire station and turn him in. He's in good health and cute as a button. Or so I heard."

The squeal that Toby made had him telling Caleb they would go and see him. After telling him that he'd call for them to make sure they didn't have any trouble with leaving with him, too, Sebastian didn't even bother telling him that he wasn't that far ahead yet. Toby was nearly dragging him out of the house and to the car.

Chapter 3

Tucker watched the doorway. Toby was sure taking her time in coming to see him, he thought. But then, he'd told her not to come back anymore, and she might well not show up. It hadn't occurred to him until just then that this might happen. Things had to be taken care of, and he wanted it done so that he could rest in peace. Like, he thought, that was going to be an option for him. Nothing was ever cut and dry anymore. There was forever some shits that wanted things to go his way. People. He hated them all.

Nightmares no longer plagued him nowadays. Thankfully. He'd get one now and then, just a little bit of the day that his beloved Hester had been taken from him along with their son and his family. Wiping at the tears that usually accompanied any thoughts that he had about that day, Tucker put his hankie away and looked out the window.

A woman and a man were headed this way

with a child. Who would bring a kid to this place, he wondered. Nothing here but dying old people who have been abandoned by their families. They must want to get in good with someone with money. He supposed if they were bringing in a kid, they'd not technically abandoned anyone, but it was a sad and depressing place. Even the ones that used to be lively around here were nothing, but skin stretched over bones, sitting in chairs until it was time for the next rotation.

"Bed, chair, dining room, chair, dining room, chair then bed. Nothing to do but sit on my ass all day and think." The woman next to him asked him who he was talking to. "Nobody. Go away."

He hated too how rude he'd become over the last ten years or so. The first…he had to think how long he'd been in here, and it occurred to him that it had been over twenty years of his sitting around on his ass and not dying like he wanted to. Next month, his son and daughter-in-law would have been celebrating their thirtieth anniversary if they'd been alive. He and his missus would have been celebrating their fiftieth the following month. It hurt him again how much he'd missed with them all. All because some kid had come into the house when he'd not been —

"You must be Mr. Hayden. May I call you Tucker?" He asked him who he was. Not even hiding the fact that he was irritated and pissed off. "The nurse up front told us that you were a bit nasty...well, she said moody, but that was right nasty of you. My name is Sebastian Gerald. I'm here with your —"

"If you're selling something, I don't have a pot to piss in. Even if I did, I'd not be dipping into it to give you a nickel. Go away and bother someone else. Actually, just go away. Nobody here wants you hanging around with them." He tried to turn his back on the man, but he held his wheelchair so it wouldn't move. "What do you think you're doing? Let me go. I'm going to report you."

"Good. You're a nasty sort of fella, aren't you? I'm here with Toby. You remember her, don't you? The nice person in the family?" That gave him pause. "We were married today, and since you called to have her come here, we thought that this would be a good time to tell you."

"You aren't married to nobody, kid. She's hopefully smart enough not to take you on so that you drain her dry, either. And I said to leave me alone." Sebastian told him to look in the doorway. As much as he didn't want to look, the man turned him so that he had no choice in the matter. The woman with a large bag of something was smiling in his direction. Her face shocked him to his core. "She could be my Hester's twin. My god, how did I miss that?"

"You told her not to come back because you were hurting too much and wanted to die. She was a kid, you asshole. And needed her grandda." He was jerked around again to face the man. "You hurt her, old man, and I will not hesitate to put you in that grave you so want to be in. She's having a good day today, and don't you dare fuck this up."

He found himself impressed with the man. Angry, too, but impressed that he had no trouble threatening him to protect Toby. As soon as his chair was released again, he turned to watch Toby coming across the room. She laid her bundle in his arms, and he couldn't help but stare at her.

"Hello, grandda. Play any chess lately?" That was all it took for him to feel all of the last twenty years weigh down on his heart. She was beautiful. Tall, like her dad, and just as beautiful as her momma had been and his Hester. "Don't cry, Grandda. Please? I brought you something."

Everything about his life came crashing down over him. The years he'd spent alone. The times that he hurt so bad, had he a gun, he would have ended it all. The holidays were the worst. No one, not a single person to share it with. Even cooped up with all these people, no one wanted to spend it with you. Because he'd been a bastard to everyone. And still was, he supposed.

"I was a fool, honey. Such a fool. I had you come here because I was going to tell you that the will is finalized and that I was going to…then you show up here with this man, and I'm about as befuddled as I've ever been. I shouldn't have sent you packing. Oh honey, will you ever —"

The bundle on his lap started to squirm, and he was fearful it was a puppy. While he liked dogs, he knew that having one of them here would have all the people here all over him for a pet or two. He'd seen it too much. But when Sebastian pulled the blanket down, he could only stare at the child laying there.

"His name is Kelly Gerald. Did Sebastian tell you that we were married? This little guy is going to be ours today, too. And I couldn't believe it when I heard his name. Kelly Tucker. Just like your middle name and my little brother's. Remember him?" The little guy took his finger into his hand and continued to stare at him. "We didn't get a chance to change his clothing out for something more appropriate for visiting his great grandda for the first time. But we got him some things on the way here. Just let me get him into something nicer, Grandda."

When she picked Kelly up off his lap, he wanted

to snatch him back to him. But a low growl from Sebastian had him stopping. Toby was still talking while he watched her take off the little sleeper that Kelly had on, then put a pair of jeans and a tee shirt on him. It was all he could do not to beg her to let him touch his warm skin. To count his little toes and fingers. He looked at Sebastian when he said his name.

"His parents couldn't raise him, so they took him to the hospital. My brother told us about him, and we went over to pick him up. It was never a question about us not taking him home with us but how quickly we could get him in our car." Tucker nodded, his heart beating so fast and hard he was afraid to speak. "She's worried that you called her in here to tell her you were going to die or something like that. You're not now, are you?"

"I don't think so." He looked at Kelly when he was cooing and smiling at him. "Is he really my great-grandson? I mean, please tell me this isn't a joke. I don't think that my heart could take it."

"He's ours, Grandda." Toby handed the baby to him again, and he held him so that they were eye to eye. "We have a lot to learn about being parents with a son, but I believe we can get through it. The name was the one that his parents gave him, so we decided not to change it. Only his last name. But we're going to have one of the rooms fixed up for him tomorrow."

"Not Little Tucker's room." She looked so sad for a second that he glanced at Sebastian to see if he was going to hurt him. "He needs his own space, I think. A room that he can grow into don't you think there, Kelly? A room with a view, too. So you can see the birds and animals that come out of the woods in the evening. Oh my, that's the ticket. A place that will be all yours in that big old house."

"That's an excellent idea, Tucker." He didn't know why, but Sebastian's approval of the room choice made him feel like he and the young man could be friends. "You should have seen us getting him clothing to wear here. Then, on the way here, Toby was buying things online for him. I had to tell her that he'd grow out of things pretty quickly at this age."

"Yes, they do tend to grow fast." He looked at Toby. "You're all grown up too, aren't you, child? The spitting image of your grannie. My goodness, I'm going to have such tales to tell her when I join her."

"Is that going to be soon, grandda? I don't want to think about you leaving me, too. I've never wanted that. But I suppose I can understand your pain. It took me a long time to get right with my own pain." He asked her if she was still living in the family home. "Yes. Sebastian and I are. I've had it redone since the murders. Dad's office is now a library. Remember how he never wanted books in there? I took the solarium down to the basics and have been fiddling with some of Mom's orchids. Mostly, Sebastian and I hang out on the back deck in the evening. We'll be having to have the windows put in soon."

"Hester, she loved that room so much." Sebastian said that he did as well. "I bet this little fella will enjoy it too. It's a good home, solid."

"Are you going to come and live with us, Tucker?" He nearly told him no and snapped at him that he just wanted to die. But the look he got from the other man had him rethinking everything. Then he looked down at Kelly.

He was staring at him like he was wondering the same thing. Like, are you going to be there for me when I scrape my knees? Learn how to walk? Are you going to be there to tell me about my grandparents, uncle, and great-grannie? Tears filled his eyes as he thought about his wife and family.

"They were murdered. I know you know that, but since that day I woke up in the hospital, I've let myself think that I was murdered, too. That little Tucker was just too young to have been killed, much less the way that it was done to him." He picked up Kelly and held him close to his heart, not looking at either of the adults with him. "My son, he wasn't perfect, and his wife, well, we had our go-arounds too. But it was me that I felt the most sorry for. Like I'd been the only one that lost out on the lives that were taken just from me. It never, not once, occurred to me that there would ever be a child that would come along. It was… he wasn't anything that I factored into my life when I was thinking about my own self. When I think back at all the years that—" He looked at Toby. "I did you the most wrong, child. Never wanting to see you or have you come around. I only just realized that I don't know a durn thing about you. Not nary a tale that I can tell this little man that you did. I did this all to myself, and I hate myself for it."

He started crying, and when Toby took Kelly from him, it was the arms of the other man that he fell into. Deep sobs, tearing his heart open for all the stupidity that he'd done. The years and years that he lost and would never be able to get back. Just sitting here while life, that of his only living relative, went on, and he'd stayed in the hate that he'd had when that young man had pulled out an axe and chopped his family up, leaving him and Toby to live.

"You can make up for it by being around Kelly, Grandda." He looked at Sebastian while Toby continued. "I have lots of things that I can tell you about my life. I've been taking care of a lot of things since I was released from—"

"You're a good man, aren't you, son?" Sebastian told him that he thought that he was. Then he told him that he'd lost his wife and child too, a very long time ago. "I'm powerful sorry about that. I truly am. If you'd not mind any, and I'm asking this of you and only you, if you'd allow me to live out the rest of my years with the three of you. You…Toby is a good girl, but she'd tell me yes because she feels like she owes me because I'm her grandda. But you, you, I think, would tell me right off if I wasn't welcome, wouldn't you?"

"I would. I'd like to think that I'd give you a chance first. However, I will say that if you hurt either of my families, this one or my brother's, I will have no trouble dropping you right back here so that you can rot in hell." It was blunt but no less than he deserved after all this time. "You come home with us, Tucker. And I promise you that you'll be a damned sight happier than you are now. Or not. I'm not going to put up with your shenanigans. I have a wife and a son now, and they're going to be my priority from now on. As well as any more children that Toby and I have. Understand?"

"I do. Thank you." He looked at Toby, who was glaring at Sebastian. "I'd have it no other way than the way that he told me, Toby. He's right. If you'd been here before him, I would have snapped your head right off, too. And I did that to him. For no more reason than that I've turned into a bitter old man who is a rude bastard that needs a second chance in his life. And I believe Sebastian and I can be good friends. We might even be best of friends before I pass on. A while from now, I hope."

Toby was a little upset, but she got over it when they had to get the paperwork taken care of. There was a good deal more of it than he'd of thought, too, for him being able to just go home as he wanted. By dinnertime, not only was he worn out, but little Kelly was as well. They were both pretty cranky by the time they were home with his momma and daddy.

While Sebastian fixed up some dinner for the three of them, Toby fed Kelly his bottle. It was strange, after all this time, to see his only grandchild feeding his only great-grandson. It was a memory that he knew that he'd have with him for the rest of his life, too. Just watching the two of them lulled him to sleep in just a few minutes.

~*~

Sebastian half listened to the man speaking to him and Toby. He should have been paying more attention from the beginning, he supposed, but it was too late for him to catch up now. So he figured when they got home, he'd let Toby talk to him, and he would get a better understanding anyway.

When the man left them in the conference room, Toby looked at him. "You didn't hear a word that he said to you, did you? Thinking about Kelly or the fact that we're not doing anything fun?" He said both. "I thought so. It appears that your mother isn't cooperating with the police on a few things that we were able to find. Not to mention, Conner and Roger are also causing a lot of trouble as well. Not that anyone is the least bit surprised by it. They're saying that you duped them into thinking that there wasn't any money left when their mother died, and it's all your fault that the will was made out the way that it was. I don't have any idea how they came up with that story, but there you have it. The next step in this is going to be up to you. What do you want to do with the three of them? At this point, I'm game. Also, when he comes back, he's going to have information on the Roman family. There has been a shake-up since the brother was killed, and things are starting to come to a head. Strangely, nothing about you so far. Since I don't know all that much about them in the first place, I can only assume that you might know a bit of what he's talking about."

"I read it in the paper last night. The head boss,

Parker, has cancer, and he's having trouble with his sons as to who is going to take his place running the operation. It's not as large as it was when he wanted me to work for him, downsizing, I guess. The police seem to think that he's all for closing up shop, so to speak, but there isn't much to go on. The sons, three of them left, are wanting to go after the hospital that diagnosed his cancer in the first place. Mistakes were made, they're saying. There is no way that cancer would take their very wealthy father from them." She rolled her eyes, and he laughed. "Yes, well, when you think that you run it all, then you can figure you can kill the messenger when you don't like the news he's giving you and pretend like nothing happened."

"So what does he think is going to happen if he is indeed planning to close down his organization? I mean, can't his sons just do it after he's dead?" He told her what he thought. "Okay, blood promise. I've never heard of that, but I'm sure that it's something that they'd do. And since he'd make them promise on this bloodletting not to reorganize and open again, they'll do it. I don't know if that's wonderful logic or just stupidity on his part for thinking that they'll do what he made them promise to do. I don't know if you know this or not, but I don't have a great deal of trust with people."

"I have noticed that about you. And yes. It's the way they run things." She seemed to be thinking about things, so he told her what else he knew. "When you killed his brother, at first, he was pissed enough to come for you. Then he heard how you'd warned him not to touch you and to unhand you. I guess he has a daughter who read it in the newspaper about what had happened. He was, I guess, pissed off, and she blasted him for thinking that *you* were the issue. She also heard from the grapevine that I have, got on his ass about coming after me when I didn't want to work for him. Then I guess she found out that he murdered my first family."

"How the hell are you getting this? Do you have spies or something?" He told her that Parker's daughter and he had gone to school together. And up until then, she'd not known about the deaths. "I see. So, are you off the hook?"

"I don't know. She said that he wants to talk to me about some things. Dawn assures me that it's just that, a meeting to talk, but I don't trust all the easily either." Toby told him that she didn't think that she would either. "But, I did agree to meet him at his next chemo treatment at the hospital. He usually does it at home, but he's agreed to go to the hospital for more tests, or so he's told his sons. Dawn is going to be there with him, and so will I, so that we can talk without his sons knowing it. Very clandestine."

"So will I." He told her that he'd have it no other way. "Good. Also, you should understand that I'm not going to go in there without backup. I know he only wants to talk, but I don't trust any more than you do."

"So you've told me, honey." They were both laughing when the attorney returned. He told them just about everything that he'd told Toby, and he gave him the little information that he had, too, with the exception of the meeting. That, he figured, was best to keep quiet about. "So what will we do now about my family?"

"For now, they're all in jail. I'm thinking that is the best place for them. Also, the house that your mother was getting from the government is being gone over with a fine tooth comb. They're finding all kinds of things there that they didn't know she was doing. They found prescription drug pads, and that is the biggest thing that is going to have her in prison for a long time. She would take them into different pharmacies around the state and pick up about a hundred of them a month to the tune of about fifty dollars because she was using the government insurance to get a deep discount on them. Then, she'd sell them online. There was a chart in one of the other bedrooms as to where and when she was to pick up the next prescription. For being as dumb as she seems, she was organized."

"I wouldn't have any idea. I never spent much time with her." The attorney, he couldn't remember his name off the top of his head, said that he was sorry. "Don't be. I had a good life for a while. Grannie loved me, and she made me the man that I am today. While I don't care what happens to any of them, however, I don't want to have to keep looking over my shoulder for the rest of my life."

"I'm working on that for you too. Also, Conner is causing trouble, the younger of the three of them, as I said. He keeps saying that he had nothing to do with the death of his father. However, evidence shows that not only did he have a large part in his death, but his, along with the other two's fingerprints are all over the weapons used. Roger, he's an ass of the highest order if you ask me. He's claiming that he has money, so he should be able to buy himself out of what is going on. Bribery is what that's called. Anyway, he's set to have his attorney come and talk to me in the next couple of days to make out a deal. I have an idea what is going to happen, but for now, I'm going to just pretend that I don't have all this other information. Your mother, she's going to prison. Even if there wasn't a trial being set up, she'd go. What she was doing to the government was way beyond any kind of way for her to make restitution. She's made her bed and — money. I nearly forgot. There is money that she had, too. All of it filled up a queen-sized mattress that was in one of the rooms at the house. She just split the sucker open and stacked money in it. As far as I know, it's not been counted as yet. But it's going to be an ungodly sum of money."

"I don't want it." The attorney, his name was Bill Fredick, he only just remembered, said he had also figured that too. "When we have an amount, we'll, I don't know, set it up for some kind of scholarship program or something. Not in her name. Just…we'll talk about it."

After finishing up with the other tasks they'd had going on, the two of them went home to get her grandda and son. It wasn't really a cause for celebration, but that was fine too. Anything they could do as a family was great to him. He'd been without very many people in his life for a very long time.

Sebastian thought that things, for now, were going in the right direction, and he was ready to be finished up with both the issues. He was also helping out with the issue that was going on with Raven's client, Mrs. Pastor, who had been killed along with the limo driver when the three of them decided to — well, he supposed it was just the older of the three of them decided that his way of getting money was much easier than being nice to his own mother when she was alive. Raven had gotten one of her sons an attorney, and tomorrow morning, they were going to find out what was going to happen to Donald. He had a feeling that the man was going to be all right, but then stranger things had happened of late.

"What do you say to helping me find some of the things in storage, Sebastian?" He asked Tucker what that might be. "Well, to be honest with you, it's been so long, I'm not entirely sure what might be stored in some of the places that, as a family, we rented out. I believe that we own these places, but I guess I need to check with Toby to see." He asked her what she knew about them.

"I know that the fees are paid monthly on the ones that we don't own. It's been on my list for a while to get into them to see what it is that we're storing. I do know that one of them is entirely full of Halloween decorations for the yard. Remember that, Grandda? How all out they'd go on that holiday?" He laughed and told her that he did now. "There is one for Christmas as well, I think. Might even be two of those." Toby had been holding Kelly, and she smiled. "We should make a trip out there before the next holiday. I think that the town would really enjoy seeing all the old decorations — if they still work and are usable — out in the yard again. He might be too young for them this year, but by next, Kelly would be ready to see them."

"My grannie lived too far out for us to have treaters. But she'd go into town and sit on the porch of a friend of hers to hand out the big candy bars. There weren't that many younger kids in our town, mostly high schooler and their parents. But the few kids they'd get would be happy with the treats." He laughed. "Then the next day, Grannie and I would start cutting down the pumpkins that didn't sell and making pumpkin everything. From cookies to pumpkin logs, my favorite."

"Did you help her hand out candy, son?" He told Tucker that he'd gone out with the other kids to have fun. Then, the year he'd turned fourteen, he'd been hurt and couldn't walk for a couple of years. "Your mother did that to you, didn't she?"

"Yes. I won't go into detail, but she took me from school on the pretense that her mother had died. Then she drugged me up so that I could live with her so she'd not be in trouble for not having the right amount of children in the house for her government card. Also, that's when she kidnapped or just after, she took Daisy from the hospital parking lot just after killing her parents. Anyway, when it was obvious that she really didn't need me, nor was I going to cooperate with her by lying, I was tossed from a moving car—going thirty miles per hour in front of the emergency room. If not for the fast-acting nurses who were out there on a smoke break, I might well have died. It was touch and go there for a while if I would make it."

"I'm so sorry to hear that. I am." Tucker looked around the little restaurant and then back at him. "You just never know what someone has had done to them until you ask. I mean, look around here. I wonder how many of the people here have gone through, if not worse then about the same as our two families have. And come together stronger. Not many people can— and I would have been one of them that didn't come back after a tragic event."

"That's what my commanding officer used to tell me. Until you walk in someone else's shoes, you can't begin to imagine what their life is like on the inside." The mood was being squashed, and he changed the subject or brought it back to the good things. "I have to go and take care of a few things with Caleb in the morning, so how about in the afternoon, we go to the Halloween storage unit and see what we have for the yard. If that's all right with you, Toby."

"Of course. It'll be a blast. And good memories, too. Even if we have to toss it all out, I'm all for going all out like my parents did for the holidays." He realized in that second that he had, at some point, fallen in love with Toby. It rendered him speechless for several minutes. "Are you all right, Sebastian?"

"Never better, as a matter of fact." He kissed her on the cheek and then took Kelly from her so that she could enjoy her meal. "You, little man, are going to be the best kid. And not at all spoiled."

They were all laughing still when they left the restaurant. Kelly had only been with them for less than forty-eight hours, and he already had more toys than he could ever play with. Yes, he was going to be the best kid, but then, Sebastian thought that he had the best of everything. A wife, son, and a good Grandda to all three of them.

Chapter 4

Donald couldn't sleep. He knew that in the morning, he was going to go to the courthouse again, but he was terrified. His brother and sisters were shouting threats at him. Mostly about him not being a team player. That he was a traitor to his country and family. While he didn't understand the country part, he was terrified that they'd catch him unawares. That was how William loved to ambush people—and beat him so that he'd not be able to have his own trial like he wanted. Not even the threat of the other three being put in solitary confinement was keeping them from scaring the daylights out of him.

"Mr. Pastor?" He said that was him. Asking the man standing outside of his cell what time it was, he said it was just a little after six in the morning. "I've been asked by Mr. Palmer to come in early to talk to you. I'm going to go over some things with you for your court appearance. You'll be going in alone, without your family, I mean to this one, as your other family members have their own time to be there."

He couldn't help it. He broke down. He had been doing that a great deal lately. His fear of them getting him in the courtroom or on the way there had been fixed so that he'd be safe. The officer that he'd only just noticed asked him to go back to the wall, and they'd go to an office to talk. Donald was never so glad that he'd been able to get away from his family as he was at that moment.

"Come on now, Donald. We have a lot to discuss, and while I feel happy for you to be away from them, we need to get this finished up. All right?" He told the man he was sorry. "No, don't be sorry. I've been reading up on some of the accounts that sent you to the hospital when you were younger up until a week before you were involved in the accident."

They were taken to a nice room, and he was given his breakfast. It was his next most favorite thing since his momma's apple pie. Sausage gravy over biscuits with cheese sprinkled all over the top of it. Somebody must have told the man that because he'd never said a word to anyone else about how that was his momma's breakfast for him on his birthday. He realized then, like he did a lot of things lately, that he never properly thanked her for going out of her way to make it for him.

Instead of getting all sloppy again, he ate his breakfast and answered questions that were put to him.

"He thought killing off Raven would be a good thing. That we'd get all the money because she was the one that was keeping momma from us having it. I've been thinking on that, and I don't know how he thought that was going to happen. When Momma had her mind set on something, there was no turning her around to your way of thinking." The other man told him that he didn't either. "She never raised her voice when she was making her point either. I think that's what made her so scary. She'd just talk to you in that momma voice of hers, and you couldn't help but obey her. I liked obeying her. But the others? Well, they would egg her on until she near slapped them into the following week."

"Well, we get through this today. Mr. Palmer will be in the courtroom with you. I'm going to be with him to help with the questions that are asked. You just tell the judge like you have me, and you'll be just fine." He wasn't entirely sure how that was to work since he knew he was a big dummy head. But he'd do what he was told.

The trip to the courthouse was nice. He'd not had to ride in the jail bus but in a real car. There were so many buttons on the thing that he had to sit on his hands, so he'd not push some of them. It sure was nice to be able to feel like a real person again. Donald thought that if he only had a little bit of jail time, he was going to use his time there to try and learn a skill. He needed a job, and he needed to know how to do it. His momma had wanted that for him, and he'd been too dumb to figure out a job when she'd wanted him to.

After rising and sitting, something that he thought was kind of funny, he was asked to stand again by the judge. Nervous as all get out, he glanced around the room and saw Raven and all her family. Waving at them, just to say 'Hey,' he was asked to pay attention.

"Mr. Pastor, I've been given a great deal of information on all the things that your family has been up to under the leadership of your brother and oldest sister. It's small wonder to me that none of you have been in prison as much as you already have been." He didn't understand some of the stuff the judge said, but told him that they'd all been in jail at some point. "Yes, exactly. Now. I've talked with the Anderson family as well as Ms. Raven. She is willing to sponsor you after your sentencing so that you won't have to go to jail. You'll spend—"

Donald's knees just gave out. If not for the seat behind him just then, he'd of surely hit the floor. As it was, he needed help from Mr. Palmer to not just get up but to stand upright, too. The judge asked him if he was all right.

"I am. I surely am. And while I messed up in letting you talk the rest of your sayings, I want you to know that I'll work hard and not have a thing to do with the others. I've been thinking on all the stuff we'd been doing, like you said, with my brother in charge, and we weren't none of us all that good. I'm going to change my ways and learn how to do something that will get me moving. And to get me a bit of pocket money so's when I want something like some French fries or something, I can pay for them instead of trying to steal them." The judge said that was what he wanted to talk to him about. "Good. I'm ready to listen now. I'm powerful sorry that I fell over just then. I'm gonna listen now."

"All right. Ms. Raven is going to sponsor you with the rest of her family in getting you on the right track with a job and a place to live. I've been told that you cannot live on your own as you have some disabilities that will prevent you from being in a safe environment if you were to live alone. Is that right?" He said he nearly burnt down the house once because he couldn't read the instructions on his apple pie. "Yes, that's what I'm talking about. So you're going to be assigned to a group home where you will not just learn a skill you can do on your own but also learn how to take care of your own needs. You will, as you said, not have any contact with your brother and sisters."

Donald listened to the judge as much as he could. But he kept getting distracted by some of the big words he was using. Whispering in his ear, Mr. Palmer told him that he'd explain to him later what he needed to do.

Donald couldn't help it, he felt good about things. Even knowing that he was a big dummy didn't bother him so much because no one was making fun of him. And he was going to be away from the family. When the judge told him that he had to go back to the jail to get the paperwork taken care of, he thought he could have just sprouted wings and flown there like a bumble bee. He was so happy. Just as he was getting in the car again, the jailhouse bus pulled up, and he got to see the other three.

April—he had to keep reminding himself that he wasn't going to call them by both their names anymore—looked just terrible. Her hair was all messy like she'd not run a good comb through it in months. Momma would have been so embarrassed at her looks and snatched her bald for going out in public that way. And she looked like she had put on some fat, too. Her jumper thingy was too tight around her belly area, and her feet were in them floppy shoes that he'd been wearing in the shower since he'd been in jail. Donald was sort of ill with the look of her feet. Like she'd been walking through food all the time and not bothered with soap and a rag.

Besty didn't look all that much better. But her hair was combed out and pulled back in some kind of flowery thing. She didn't have on a jumper suit but was wearing the clothes that she'd had on the day they'd been arrested. He had a thought that April couldn't fit in her own clothing no more, so that's why April was in the jumper thing. Not that it did her any good about what she was wearing. It was dirty and wrinkled up like she'd not even bothered with putting an iron to it.

It was his brother who looked the worst. He'd put on a lot of fat since he'd seen him last time. Not only did he have himself a wobbler of a neck, as momma would have called it, but he also had fat hands and legs. His momma would be like that at the end of a gardening day. All swelled up with her legs burning. William, too, had on a jumper thing, but the color of it, bright orange, made him look like one of the road cones that he remembered his brother running down and making them flop in the air when he'd see them. Good heavens, he thought that he might be the dumbest of them all, but he'd been taking care that he made sure that he didn't look like the dummy he thought he was.

"Have you seen enough?" He looked over at Mr. Palmer when he asked. "I have some news for you about your family, Donald. They're going to prison, the three of them. Since they wanted to be tried as one, they're going to go down for the homicide of the limo driver and your mom. They'll get life if I don't miss my bet without any chance of parole. The other things, there were seven more murders that they're all going to be tried for, will add additional life terms onto their sentencing that will keep them in there for the rest of their natural life. William will be tried as well for the abuse of his children."

"He don't have no children." Mr. Palmer told him that he had four. And that he'd been abusing them since birth. "I didn't know that. Are they going to be all right? I don't want them to suffer because William wasn't a good man."

"They're going to be just fine now. They're being taken care of, thanks to Caleb and Tabby Anderson. They'll not come here but will be living out a better life than the one that they currently have. An education, too, will be there if they wish it. You're not to have contact with them, however. The judge thinks that it will be hard on them knowing that you're related to them through their father." He nodded, watching his brother fighting with the officer, trying to get him out of the bus. "Once they're set up for a trial, if it comes to one—they want the judge to just tell them how much they'll owe so they can kill Raven to get it all to pay the fines—then they'll be finished being bad as William had promised him. No trial means that they'll go straight to prison from here and not be heard from again."

"I'm a lucky man, ain't I, Mr. Palmer?" He said that he was very lucky. "Thank you for this. And I'll be sure to thank Ms. Raven, too. She did me a lot of good in calling you, and I'll never be able to repay her for this."

"You just keep with the program, Donald, and you'll repay her a great deal. She's a good woman, and your mother was very lucky to have had her. Once you get to where you're going, you keep telling yourself that. You were a lucky man, and try to help someone else out with your luck." He asked him if that was paying it forward. "It is. You keep paying it forward, and that will be more than thanks to young Raven."

After all the paperwork was finished up, it was nearly noon time. As he stood out in front of the jailhouse with his face up to the sun, he thought of the first thing that he was going to do. He was going to buy him his first meal out on the town. Donald made his way to the Dari Twist that was just across the road and stood in line. He was never so nervous or happy in his entire life that he was a free man and had pocket money to boot.

"Can I buy you lunch?" He hugged Ms. Raven when she spoke to him. "I just got off the phone with Mr. Palmer. He said that he saw you coming over here. Come on, we'll have us a nice lunch, then we'll talk."

It was a great lunch, and he'd never been so happy for the company as he was if it was his own momma sitting with him. Ms. Raven was pretty, too. She made him feel like a real man when she asked him where he wanted to sit. He didn't remember anybody asking him where he wanted to stand, much less sit with them.

"Here." She handed him a big envelope and told him to go through it while she put catsup on her fries as soon as they sat down. The first thing he found was money. "That's for you to get yourself some new clothing as well as the personal things that you need. Harlin, my husband, is going to help you with that as soon as you're ready. Also, there is a cell phone that is yours. I want you to call me whenever you want so that if you have any questions, you can get them answered. All right?"

"Yes, ma'am." He fingered the cell phone but put it away. "I don't know how to use it, but it sure is pretty, don't you think? I'll make sure that someone teaches me so I can call you if I need you."

"Good. That's another thing that I wanted to tell you. Don't be ashamed to ask for help or to tell someone that you don't understand something. You're going to need to learn a lot of things over the next few months, and not asking when you need help will only delay your progress." He nodded as he bit into his hamburger. "I also wanted to tell you that so long as you are following the program, I'll make sure you have money in your account. After you start getting paid for working, then you will be just fine."

"Thank you for that. They said to me that I'd not be around here. Where am I going?" She told him that it was still in Ohio but about three hours from here so that he could get a fresh start." He nodded and then remembered what she'd said to him. After telling her that he didn't know what that meant, she smiled at him. "It means that no one will know about your family where you're going, and that will help you with making friends. You don't have to tell anyone anything you don't want to. Remember that. You're on your own, and what you tell people or not is up to you."

"I don't know that I want anyone to know about

my family." She said that was up to him. "You've been so nice to me, Ms. Raven. I know you want me to pay it forward like Mr. Palmer told me, but I want you to know that I'm going to make you proud of me from now on. I'm going to be a good man like my momma wanted me to be when I was a little kid. You won't have no trouble with me. I promise.

"You just have a good life and be a good man, and that will make me as happy as I can be." When Harlin showed up, he told him what was going to be going on and showed him the cell phone. He felt like a big dummy head again when he realized that the man would know he'd gotten it, but he never made him feel that way. He even showed him how to turn it on and how to dial numbers. It was the best day of his life, he thought, but he was going to try his bestest to have more of them every day, just for his momma and Ms. Raven.

~*~

Sebastian hadn't been this tired since his first day in the service. His body ached. Once he was up in his room, of course, he couldn't lay his head down on his pillow if he had wanted. He was, for the most part, hyped up and feeling antsy. Going to the window that showed him the backyard, he watched the night creatures that roamed the grounds. He couldn't wait for him and

Kelly to be able to sit right here and wait for them to come out. He'd make sure that not only did he know the names of the animals but that he was able to tell him what they sounded like.

Thinking about Kelly, he made his way across the room to his bedroom. The night nanny was on duty tonight so that they could both get some sleep. But after thinking of the little guy, he decided that sleep was the furthest thing from his mind. Creeping quietly down the hall so as not to disturb the household, Sebastian paused when he heard a slight whimpering sound.

Since he was new to the house, he couldn't quite pinpoint where the noise was coming from. Cocking his head while standing outside the baby's room, he heard it again. That's when he realized it was coming from the end of the hall where Toby's room was.

Running and leaping at the door, he did something that he'd not done since he'd been out of the service. Hitting the door with both feet, rolling and tumbling into the room, had him coming up on his feet quickly. Without a weapon, he wasn't sure what he could do, but he looked around the room until he found the source of the noise.

Not seeing Toby at first, he looked at the doorway when Tucker asked where she was. It took them both a little too long to find her before he went to her. As soon as he spotted the bundle huddled tightly against the dresser that was near the window in her room, he made his way there, careful of the broken things as well as the items that were strewn across the room. Touching her shoulder had her coming up from the floor and attacking him immediately.

"I have you. Baby, I have you." She fought him for a few more minutes until she finally went limp in his arms. Picking her up, he sat down on her bed and held her while she cried. Gut-wrenching sobs that tore at a part of him yet untouched before. Once her grandda came to her, he watched the couple in the doorway. "I have her. She must have had a bad dream."

Ginger came into the room and started picking up the broken items Toby must have fallen into trying to get away from her night terrors. After telling her and Herman that he'd get it in the morning, he shooed them off to bed. It wasn't long before Tucker himself sat down on the chair by the bed.

"I wonder if she has these nightmares all the time." Sebastian told him that he'd been there a month now and he'd not heard her. "That's good. I'd hate to think that she goes through this every night. Poor little mite. I hate that she had to go through this at all."

Sebastian rocked Toby back and forth, telling her over and over that he had her. That he'd not let anyone hurt her again. Tucker would comment, too, telling his granddaughter that he was there for her and that he should never have left her in favor of wallowing in his own misery.

"You didn't do anything wrong, Grandda. I just sometimes have bad thoughts that take over." When she sat up in his arms, Toby looked at him. "You saved me just now. I don't know how, but without you coming to my aide tonight, I don't think that I would have — I was going to jump from the window."

"Don't do that." He touched his fingers to her cheek. "Please don't do that. I don't know what I'd do —" Sebastian looked into her face. "I've fallen in love with you, Toby. It just occurred to me how I don't believe that I could survive without you near me or with me either. You've owned my heart since...I think we'll before I thought of having someone in my life. But here you are. Here for me, and I don't want to live without you and Kelly in my life. And, of course, Tucker. We're going to be a good family together."

"I love you too." He held her tightly to his chest and watched Tucker pull out his handkerchief and wipe his eyes. Toby laughed a little before speaking. "You were forever with a hankie, Grandda. I remember thinking that it was magical in some way. You could get James to laugh with it by making little creatures with it when he'd scrapped his knee. Even used it to clean up his little boo-boos when he had one. Oh, and I remember once when we were at that Italian restaurant, you made him a kerchief like the cooks and waiters were wearing. I want you to show Kelly every one of those magical powers. All right?"

"Yes. Oh yes, I can do that. I'd forgotten about all those times until just this minute. Oh, what fun we'd have." Tucker laughed again before he put his hankie away. "I used to do the same thing with your daddy. I did. He'd be upset about one thing or another, and then all I'd have to do was pull out one, and he'd be calmed down and watch me. I think he called it magical as well. Toby, honey, thank you for that memory." He smiled; it was a watery smile, but Sebastian thought it was a happy one. "We should do that more often. Talk about the good times rather than dwelling on that one day. Yes, sir. I'm going to do that from now on. Get myself out of the funk that I was in. I'll find you when I have me a good memory of your parents or little James. Even your grandma, too. Oh, what fun times we used to have around here. Surely you remember some, too, Toby. Don't you?"

"Yes. The time that Mom and Dad hosted that cheese and wine party. You filled James and me up a plate of different cheeses and crackers." Tucker started laughing hard before Toby had finished. "Yes, I can see you remember it too." She looked at him. "That was the most vile crap I've ever tasted. Oh, James and I were sick for a week, it felt like. Nasty cheeses that came from all over the world, and we couldn't understand why anyone would care. Oh, and Dad making fun of the three of us for thinking we'd gotten away with something. I don't think I've had cheese since without thinking about that day."

They talked about that party and many more that had been held in this house. The antics of them getting around their parents when it came to the holidays. Tucker told them of the day that he'd proposed to his wife. There was a story about the day that James had been brought home from the hospital. How he'd seemed so tiny to them all.

"He fit right in the palm of my hand. Almost afraid that I'd crush him when I sneezed that time." Tucker laughed. "But he was a good little boy. Didn't give anyone a bit of trouble when he was growing up. I miss that lad. I surely do."

"I do as well." Everyone turned to Toby when she spoke. "The man that killed him. I found out later that he was suffering from depression. He thought that having it all, as in a non-job that he didn't have to come to work for, would please his parents in some way. But he'd already killed them before coming to our home that night. From what I've been able to figure out, he'd had such a hard life because no one believed that he could be as depressed as he said he was. That since he'd been found the one time when he'd tried to end his life, he'd been wanting attention and nothing more. I began to feel sorry for him and the people like him. There is funding for people like him now that I've set up. They can, and they do get the kind of help that makes it so that they have someone there with them at all times. It's named for my parents."

"That's a right nice thing to do, honey. You tell me all the details, and I'll help out with that. Depression is a nasty disease. I know that firsthand. But at least I had people around me all the time who understood what I was going through so they could help me out when I needed it." Tucker stood up then. "Well, I think this old man has had enough excitement for one night. I love you two. And that little boy down the hall. You, the three of you, saved me. That day, you were coming there to show me little Kelly. I want you to know that I was going to end my life that night. I'd been saving up my medication, and I was going to take it all at one time." He laid three handfuls of pills on the bedside that was beside him. "There they all are. I've no intention of letting myself get there again. Not now.

I have a family. One that I've had all along but I never once thought of…well, I'm thinking right now, and I know how to get myself together. Even if it's to take a short walk out in the town. I promise you both, I won't do anything like what I'd been thinking."

When he walked away, his hankie coming out of his pocket again, Sebastian looked at Toby. She laid her head on his shoulder while she watched the door close behind her grandda. When she got up off his lap and began cleaning up the pills, he grabbed the trashcan. He told her that they shouldn't flush them, but they couldn't leave them laying around either.

"No. I know that Kelly isn't big enough to get to them. But I don't want to leave them out either." Once they were finished with the clean-up, he put them in a paper bag that Toby found for them. "I'll take them to the pharmacy to have them disposed of in the morning. Well, I guess today. Are you all right?"

"To be honest, I feel wrung out but better mentally than I have in a while." He told her good. "Will you hold me tonight? I need you there for me."

"Absolutely. So long as it's not this bed. It's too small for my frame." They held hands as they entered Kelly's nursery, then again when they made their way to the master suite. "This room is so lovely. I have been trying to figure out a way to have you share it with me for days now."

"I've been avoiding you somewhat." He turned to her and asked why. "Because I wasn't sure that you were in love with me too. I, like you, have been falling in love with you for so long. It's like I don't remember a part of my life that you weren't there or needed to be there."

He pulled her into his arms and then to the bed. After she was in the middle, he crawled in behind her, feeling her warmth all over himself. Once they were about as close as two people could get, he wrapped his arms around her and pulled her closer still. She was asleep in seconds. Sebastian wasn't too far behind her, either.

Chapter 5

Toby wasn't keen on hospitals. It had been a place that had never been high on her list of places to go. Not even if a friend was there. But today was something that she was going to do so that they could get this thing with the Roman family behind them. Going to the chemo floor, she was able to spot Mr. Roman, Parker, right away. She sat down in the chair next to him. It was then that she noticed that they were the only three people on the floor.

"You're not going to be hurt. I promise you." She asked Parker why she should believe him. "Because, even for what I've been all my life, I'm a man of honor. I will not allow you to be harmed while we're here. I promise you on the heart of my mother."

"You said while we're here. Can I expect to be gunned down when we're out of here? If so, you're going to be gone before you get all that drug into your system, Mister. I'm not one to fuck with." He said he wasn't either and no, she'd not be gunned down by anyone because he didn't want her dead. "I don't either. I've only just found out I'm in love with someone, and I have a son of my own."

"Congratulations then. I'm very happy for the two of you." She thanked him. "I don't wish to cause you any harm, and I am profoundly sorry that my brother harmed you. And pushed you to the point that you needed to end his life. I have seen the video of him grabbing you. Our mother she would have wrapped his head around a pole had she seen him touching you in such a way." Toby asked him if she had forgiven her as well. "Yes. She wished that it hadn't come to death for him, but she understands and says that she might well have done the same thing. Only he'd not been given the chance as you gave him. He knew better."

"He should have. I warned him twice not to touch me and to unhand me. It was his fault that he chose to ignore a woman when she said no." He laughed a little, then smiled at her. "You have more to say, I take it?"

"I do. However, you're refreshing to me. Not many people who know who I am and what I am disagree with me. Nor do they challenge me as you have done. Killing my brother was quick and justified for you. The only other thing that I can tell you, Ms. Gerald, is that I respect you. You came here not knowing what I had planned, and that makes me think that you're braver than even I am."

"I've lost a great deal of people in my life. Most of my loved ones before I was very old. You learn to respect less and less as you begin to understand that most all people are only out for one thing and one thing only. Your brother was one of those kind of people." He nodded. "You, however, aren't. You give as you get, and you question before acting. That's the kind of person that I think I'd like to be thought of as well. While your brother is dead, it was of no fault of my own. He knew the consequences before he was killed by me."

"He did. And that is the main reason that I have no desire to have you killed. You were respectful in giving him an option. While he gave you none at all. Which brings me to your husband." Parker turned to Sebastian. "I have a feeling that should I harm you in any way, Sebastian, your wife will not hesitate in ending my life — though much slower — just as she did my brothers. Won't she?"

Toby didn't speak but laid the gun that she'd been able to get past the guards on Parker's lap. He didn't reach for it but did laugh. Like her being able to sneak the gun in had been a treat for him. When he reached for her hand and kissed the back of it, she let him lace his fingers into hers. When he laid his head back on the chair he was sitting in, she looked at him.

"I'm dying. If I make it home today, it will be my last trip anyway, but to the funeral home. I've known that this would be my last few days on this earth since yesterday. It saddens me greatly that I have no time to get to know you and your family, Sebastian." Sebastian asked him what he needed for him to do. "There is nothing you can do. Even the doctors, who keep telling me I have as much time as I need, haven't any more tricks up their sleeves. I believe, as I told your wife, they are keeping on my good side so that I don't harm them or their family. I shan't do that. I'm an old man with cancer. Not the monster they believe me to be."

"Does your family know?" Parker shook his head. "I see. So you came here instead of resting at home with your family around you to what end? Surely you don't expect me to do the deed for you, do you, Parker?"

"Good heavens, no." Parker sat up with laughter still spilling from his lips. "I had hoped I'd have another holiday or two, but that's not going to happen. Or even one of my mother's famous meals. She can cook as well as she did when she'd been in her twenties. But she does know that I might not be home today. But I have to tell you, this, just being with the three of you has given me a boost that I'd not expected."

"I'm sorry." Parker told Sebastian that he was as well. "You've taken care that myself and my sister are safe, haven't you? I don't want to be cold, but that's all I can think about is how my sister isn't going to have a good life because of the things that you've decided about me."

"It's all done now. No one will come after you or your little family. That would include your sister — who is not your sister, by the way." Sebastian told him that he knew that as well. "There is some paperwork on the two of you that I've had researched in full. Also, on the woman who claims to be your mother. She isn't in the event you didn't know that."

"I'm aware of her deceit. Also, that of her brothers." Parker leaned back on the chair again and nodded. "She's going to prison. Her and the other two for their partnership in killing off my grandfather."

"I'm going to tell you something. Something that I've done for you, young man. They'll never make it to prison. Before you get upset with me for telling you that, I'd like to tell you what I've found out that no one else will be able to. The woman of the couple that she killed when she took you was my family. My cousin Veto and his wife Carolyn Roman." Toby looked at Sebastian, surprised. "Yes, I can see by the look on your face that you'd not known that part. I hadn't either until I sent someone out to find your biological family. It was my intention to introduce you to your long-lost family today when I got news of how you were related to me. Veto, he knew that the child that his wife carried wasn't his either. But it made no difference to him. He would have raised you to be his son, and no one would have questioned him about it. Berkely raped Carolyn just after she and Veto got engaged. That, as they say, changed the entire course of the river that I was willing to let flow on. Then Heather came along and decided to tear our family up even more. When she murdered them for no other reason than greed. And today, before you leave here, if not already, she will understand what it is to mess with someone with my connections. I might well have let the men go, but they, too, had a hand in her killing them as well. My cousin and his wife they were only in their twenties, their entire lives ahead of them, when she decided to kill them and then kidnap you."

Sebastian sat down on the chair that was behind him. Parker sat up and reached for his hand. Once he had it in his own, he smiled at Sebastian, continuing his story about what it was he had found out.

"Carolyn was my godchild. Her father was my father's partner in crime, so to speak, when they were children. Carolyn was their only child, and it broke both her parents when they found her body. She had murdered them in such a way that it was difficult to understand that she was a person, much less a new mother. Even if Veto had not been related to me, I would have done the same thing because of her relationship to me." Parker eyed them both. "Are you upset with me?"

"No." Sebastian got up to pace, and when he stopped suddenly and turned to Parker, it startled them both. "You did this because you wanted me to be out of harm's way. Or have an alibi when they were killed. Which is it?"

"Both. If you remember, you were supposed to meet her this morning at the jail." Sebastian said that he had forgotten. "Yes, I thought you might have. I knew what her plans were from the start: to get you to come to the jail to bail her out. I wasn't sure you'd do it. Mother/son relationships can be tricky. But when I called you to tell you that I was going to be here this morning and it would be the only time we could meet, it was to get you here and to both give you an alibi as well as out of harm's way. Her brothers are going to be killed as well. I didn't want anything to happen to you or your lovely wife."

"So we're related. I'm not sure how to take that.

I mean, you did have my wife and child killed when I turned you down coming to work for you." He told him that he'd not done that. "You're going to tell me that Heather had something to do with that as well, aren't you? After all the things that I'm finding out about her, it wouldn't surprise me in the least bit that she did it." Parker said that the police would go over her involvement in his wife's death when they leave here. "I never thought that I would have a family around when I was a child. Now it seems as if they're coming around all over the place."

"Yes, we are a large family. And they are your family, too." He nodded, and the room was suddenly filled with men and women welcoming the two of them to the family. "I wanted them to get to know you in a way that I cannot. These are my closest relatives, and they know the story behind what happened all those years ago. If you are ever in need of anything at all, you are only to call one of them, and they'll make it happen."

Toby wasn't sure that she liked this. First of all, all the people. She didn't get along well with people in the first place. To have as many as thirty just there was almost too much. Staying where she was, she thought that she could get a handle on things much better, right up until Parker's mother came to sit beside her.

"My mother doesn't speak English well. She told me all my life that she thought it was a guttural language." Parker laughed. "But she has since changed her mind. Anyway, she would like to meet your and Sebastian's son. I'm to understand that he is here getting a checkup?"

"He is. My grandfather and he are in the cafeteria. I can call him if you want." Parker said that would be good. After calling her grandda and telling him what was going on, he said he'd join them in the room. "There are police here too. Are they here to confirm things the way you want them?"

"Yes. The staff, too. I don't want anything to happen to my new family." She thanked him. "What is your opinion of Heather and her brothers? I want you to be honest with me, young lady." She said that she wished she'd thought of having them taken care of. That had Parker laughing as hard as she'd ever heard anyone laughing. "Thank you for your honesty. I have a feeling that you would have been anyway if I'd not asked. But this is beautiful. Thank you."

They talked for a bit more. And when Kelly was brought into the room, Grandma Ramon held him for a few minutes, fussing over his little man's clothing of jeans and a small tee shirt, Parker told her until he was laid in the sick man's lap.

"I don't want to hold him too long. The chemicals they give me, I don't want him to breathe them in. But he is a handsome little man, isn't he?" Toby agreed. "Oh my, to be able to see him growing up. I've been keeping an eye on Sebastian since the day I asked him to work for me. I made a mistake in letting him believe that I had killed his wife. I should have come clean the moment it happened. But I was just finding out that I was at the end of my life, and I—well, I guess you could say I got distracted somewhat. But the police, they have all the information that he'll need or want on how it happened."

"Can you tell me? So that I can be prepared for his questions when they come?" Parker told her what he'd found out after handing Kelly back to her. "So she gets it in her head that no woman is good enough for her son because she wants him to only have her to worry about. That's the stupidest reason I've ever heard for killing a woman and her child. She's a sick fuck if you ask me."

"Oh, but you don't know the half of it. She has murdered for a good deal less than that. Money was always the biggest factor in her dealings. I've never met nor heard of a person like her. Her death will come as no surprise to many people, but the fact as to how it is told that she dies will make others know she got just what she deserved." She asked Parker how she was to die. "I can't tell you that. But I want you to be as surprised as the rest of the world will be. If that's all right with you. She was a monster, as you know. Her death and that of her brothers will go down as the most justified deaths of all time. Trust me when I tell you, she will suffer badly for her part in Sebastian's life. And that of little Daisy. Will you be bringing her home to live with you?"

"I don't know. I mean, we never got that far about discussing her living arrangements." She eyed him with a cocked brow. "You took care that she has money in her accounts, haven't you? You know Caleb's mother, too, if I don't miss my bet."

"Formidable woman, that one. Yes, I knew her. The world lost a great champion when she passed away. While I'd like to tell you we were good friends, we more tolerated each other. She knew of Sebastian and my — let's call it hold over him. She found me one night in less than good circumstances, and I ended up owing her. Not to hear her say it, but I did. So when she came to me about little Daisy and her family, she, well, she put me in the direction of finding out that Sebastian was a part of my family. And before you ask, if you were, yes, I took care that Howard Berkely hurt no more women." Toby was surprised by that. And told

Parker that. "Good. I like it when I can get something ahead of you. You're going to go far, I think, my dear, and I shall miss it."

"I'll keep you informed." They were both laughing when Sebastian brought her a large platter of food. As she was feeding herself some of the more delicate items on the plate, Parker told Sebastian what he'd done to help the world out with Berkley. When Sebastian started taking notes, she knew that he was going to take it all to Caleb. Toby thought that everyone would be happy about that information, too.

~*~

Exhaustion hadn't been as hard on him as it had been for the last several days. They were both working hard, getting things lined up and straightened out with their individual wealth. Settling up affairs about the house and joint accounts. Toby had a great deal more than he did, but it didn't bother either of them, so they just combined everything and took care of the bills together. Like a real family would do, he supposed.

"What do you know about investments?" He told Toby that he had been doing them since he'd been in grade school that his grannie had taught him. "Good. You can take over for the guy I used to use. He's retired now, and I don't want to have to mess with it if I don't have to. Unless you'd rather not."

"No, that's wonderful. I can do it easy. A few hours a day, and then I can have the rest of the day to hang out with family." When Toby went into the bathroom, he stripped down to his boxers and sat on the side of the bed. He could have fallen asleep right then, but he heard the door open behind him. Without turning, he spoke to her. "I don't think I'm ever going to be able to get over being this tired for another thirty years. Even my hair feels exhausted."

She didn't say anything, and he turned just enough to see her standing in front of the bathroom door. Turning fully to see if she really was naked, his cock stretched like it was going to track her. As she shimmied, he had no other word for how she moved across the room toward him. He watched as she sat down between his legs and pulled his boxers down.

"Are you too tired for me to do this to you, Sebastian?" She took the tip of his cock into her mouth and licked his crown. He realized then that he wasn't nearly as tired as he had thought that he was and put his hand on the top of her head. "No, don't touch me. I'm going to do things to you that will have your eyes rolling to the back of your head and your cock filling my mouth. I also want you to come all over me. Would you like that?"

He nodded, not even sure what he was agreeing

to. His mind was so centered around her being where she was. When she took his cock from his boxers, he nearly cried out when his tightly filled balls got a little pinch from her pulling the boxers down his hips. Pulling them free of his body with her help, Sebastian was sure that she had been planning this for a while. She seemed to have all her moves worked out in order to give him the most pleasure he'd ever had during sex.

She cupped his balls in her hands as she sucked on his cock. The motion of her head going up and down, like he was fucking her had him dizzy with pleasure. Each time she gave this balls a small tug, he felt the climax that was coming over him back off. Even gripping the side of the bed, tearing at the sheets beneath him, Sebastian couldn't keep up with her movements. She was, he thought, trying her best to kill him.

Her body was slick with sweat. His was, as well. The need to come was hurting him in ways that he'd never felt before. Each time she moved her mouth over his cock, he knew a whole new meaning to the phrase sucked him dry.

"Are you enjoying this?" He nodded, again not positive if he could have given her a verbal answer. "I am as well. I love the way that your cock fills my mouth. I want to feel you inside of me, too. But first, I want you to come all over me."

"Yes." She stood up then, and he pulled her close enough that he could suckle at her breasts. They were small but firm. Her nipples were tight and such a lovely shade of pink that he couldn't help but nip at the thick buds over and over. She pushed him back onto the bed, and he lay there, waiting for her to make the next move.

She sat on his thighs. Wrapping his hand around his cock, he only had to give it a single tug, and he was coming. It was a sight that made him come all the harder as his cum splashed against her lips, chin, and breasts. Christ. Then, when she rubbed his cream all over herself, he had to close his eyes. Too much. Not only that, but he thought that his head was having a brain attack.

"I want to ride you." All he could think about was that he was spent. That if she wanted to ride him, she was on her own. As he helped her settle over his cock, Sebastian thought he was about as hard it was going to be not to come right away as his body had a mind of its own. Or perhaps it just didn't care about anything but pleasing his other half. As she slowly slid down over him, his balls, already tight against his body, seemed to have grown tighter. Filled even more.

Holding her thighs as tightly as he dared, he begged her to give him a moment so that he could enjoy her.

When she moved, just to adjust her hips, he sat up and held her to him as he came. Christ, it felt like his entire body was being turned inside out and then dragged through a wormhole until he was sitting back on the bed. Rolling her to her back, she pouted at him, but at this point, it was too much. He needed to have her come with him.

Fucking her was something that he'd thought of for days. Even before that, he thought. She had been his other half. The woman that completed him. Slowing himself down, touching every inch of her that he could reach, he marveled at how soft her flesh was. How beautiful she smelled. Even her taste, a sweet sweat with the soap that she'd bathed with this morning, was more than he could have hoped for.

"I need to come." He did as well and told her just to give him a moment. "No. I need to come, and I need so desperately for you to come with me. Now, Sebastian. I need you to come with me now."

The climax that he had, that he shared with her, was more than he could have imagined. Even as his cock emptied deep within her, he could feel his body and mind connecting with her. They were one. In that moment, they were a couple. One that would spend the rest of their lives loving each other.

Sebastian fucked her through three more powerful climaxes. His body didn't want to quit. As he came a second time, his body hard against hers, he suckled at her breasts until she cried out that she was coming again. Just as he was falling back, his body spent, he rolled over so as not to crush her and fell asleep.

Waking sometime in the dark room, he reached for Toby, and she moved closer to him. Pulling her atop him, he held her gently in his arms as he drifted back to sleep. This was something that he'd been wanting all his life and hadn't known it. Someone to cuddle with and to love throughout the night.

The next time he woke up, the room was still dark, and he reached again for Toby. However, he came across a cold sheet, and she was not in the room. Getting up, he found the light on in the bathroom and knocked on the door. She told him that she was coming to bed for him to warm it up for her.

He must have dozed off waiting for her, so when she stretched her cold body next to him, he laughed. Whatever she'd been doing, it had been long enough that she felt frozen through. Holding onto her until she warmed up, he started to drift off.

"I want children with you." He told her that he'd

love that too. "I don't mean just us having them but adopting them too. I want my children to understand that money doesn't mean the end all to problems. I want them to know that we have to give as much as we can."

"I agree with you on that. Without my grannie taking me in, there is no telling how I would have turned out. The same with Kelly. Having money does have its advantages, as I'm sure you know, but as you said, it doesn't mean that it can solve all problems." She kissed him on his nose, and he laughed again. "What was that for? Not that I mind, but what was that cute kiss for?"

"For being perfect for me." He didn't think he was nearly that, but she snuggled up and under his chin, and he knew the moment she was asleep. Sebastian lay there for several minutes, thinking of having a houseful of children, and couldn't wait. Of course, they'd need to try harder now that they'd come to the decision to have children, and he couldn't wait. Moving his legs around, however, made him realize that he was going to have to rest up if they had sex like this every night. He'd be old before his time if he didn't get rest.

Waking again, the room was bright with light, and he stretched before thinking about how sore he was going to be. Looking over at Toby when she giggled, he asked her if she was sore too.

"I'm afraid to blink. I don't know if you can strain your eyeballs or not, but I feel like I'd be safer if I didn't push it." They both laughed and then moaned. "That was fantastic, don't get me wrong, but damn, I hurt everywhere. I've thought about getting up and taking a long, hot shower, but the thought of putting my feet on the floor to walk to the bathroom scares me a bit."

In the end, they helped each other to the bathroom. Even for as short of a walk as it was, they were moaning and groaning about it. As soon as they stepped under the hot spray, it was as if all the aches and pains just washed away. Pulling her into his arms, he kissed her with all the gentleness he could manage while pressing her against the shower wall.

Sebastian took her hard. His body, still spent from last night, was only able to give her as much pleasure as he could. Touching her ass, he pulled her closer to him and held her there while he moved in and out of her. It was like he'd never made love before. Not like it was with her.

"Take me, Sebastian. Please, I need to feel whole." Fucking her harder, taking her slightly savagely, he felt her body tightened around his cock and nipped none too softly at her throat. When she cried out, Sebastian came with her. His cock filled a second time before he was able to back away.

Both of them sated leaned against opposite walls of the stall and smiled. When she reached for him, it was all he could do not to cringe from her. His body was finished. If he had to run from this house because it was on fire, he'd die. That was all there was to it.

Getting out of the stall had them both making slight noises on their hurts. When she couldn't dry her hair, he did it for her. Even going so far as to have her sitting on the room's only seat, the toilet, so that he could dry her feet.

"The more I move around, the more I realize that I'm totally out of shape for you." Toby laughed. It was a hardy laugh like she'd been caught off guard by it. "I think that we should just hang out here today, play with Kelly, and not leave the couch."

"Excellent idea. I'm all for it." As soon as they dressed, both of them opting for shorts and tee shirts, he went to the nursery to get Kelly. When he turned to look at him, the little guy smiled. Sebastian thought that he could live forever on that one little toothless smile.

After an early lunch, the three of them did hang out in the living room. There was a lot that they could have been doing, but neither of them felt like moving. Even Kelly, for being as young as he was, seemed to understand that it was a fuss-less day. The three of them, well he and Toby, decided to have dinner delivered, and they even ate that on the living room floor.

All in all, he thought it was the best day that he'd had in a good long time. He was going to make more days like this with his family. Now, all he had to do was to get Daisy home with them, and he thought that he could take on the world. Maybe in a couple of days, he told himself, still hurting from making love with Toby.

Chapter 6

"Parker's mother died last night." Toby told him that she'd heard about it on the news and that the Roman family was going to put on a large street fair in their honor. "Yeah, it talks about that in the paper too. How the family is going to provide all the food and that you only needed to bring your own containers to take things home or plateware to eat there with them. Or both. That was very generous of them. The police are going to be serving up the food for them all. Nice way to bring all the family and the cops together."

"That'll help a lot of people that day and beyond. If there are any leftovers, it's all going to the shelters around the state. He was a generous man, as it turns out." Toby turned in her chair and looked up at him. "What are we going to wear to this thing? I'm assuming that we're going?"

"Yes. We were asked that we come so that more

of the family could get to know us. I'm still blown away by the fact that we're related to the Romans. Well, at least I am, and by extension, you guys, too. Do you suppose that Heather had any idea when she took me what she was doing?" Toby told him that she didn't think Heather ever knew what she was doing. "Good point. But she's gone now, and we're free to roam around without having to look over our shoulders all the time. From any of the three of them. They were monsters, the lot of them."

It hadn't been a good death for her or her brothers either. While he knew that it had been planned, it still shocked him when he was informed of the accident. It was funny to him that her demise hadn't warranted as much press as a mobster had when he passed away three days ago. Heather and her two brothers had suffered badly for their part in the killing of some of the Roman family and the kidnapping of Sebastian. And he wasn't going to lose any sleep over her death or that of her brothers. He promised himself he wasn't going to think of them ever again.

The bus that they'd been in headed to prison had been hit by a train while crossing the tracks. The driver of the train and the few people on board weren't hurt at all. The bus driver, a man who was set to retire, had died on impact. But Sebastian had heard that his family made out much better for his being killed in the line of duty rather than taking his retirement and pension. He knew what was going to happen before he got on the bus. Dying this way rather than rotting away with cancer seemed a better way to him. Sebastian was happy that things had worked out for everyone.

"Before I forget to tell you, Grandda is out in the barns looking over some of the stuff that has been stored out there. He told me that if he wasn't in by lunch, I was to send out a search party that he was lost for good." Sebastian said he'd go out there and help him. "I have a list of things that I'd like for you guys to look for besides the decorations. When my family was killed, all the furniture from my parent's bedroom was stored away for me to go through. According to the list from the attorney, there is mom's jewelry box, which it says right here is fairly large, as well as some books that my dad treasured that were put out there. If you could find them, that would be wonderful. I don't know what shape they'd be in after all this time, but I want to sell it. Or give it away. I don't need to hold onto their things to hurt when I see them." She left him to go to her office.

"We'll find them." He was just getting himself a sandwich when he heard from Toby again. She asked him to find out if there was any clothing out there. "I doubt that it would be any good after all this time. What on earth do you want those for? I suppose it's none of my business, but I'm just curious."

"Everything about my life concerns you now, too. I want you to never forget that, Sebastian. I love you." He grinned at her while eating. "They were my parents' things, and I thought that someone might get some use of the material if nothing else. I don't want them, not at all, but someone might be able to cut them down into something nicer. Like a blanket or even a prom dress. I don't know." He told her he was sorry. "Don't be. It was a strange thing to ask for. Also, there might be some of James' things out there, too. Trucks and such. Kelly might be able to play with them by next summer. The other kids as well might get some use out of them as well."

By the time he was headed to the storage barn, he had a longer list than just the few things that had been mentioned from her first thing. He was happy to see that some of his brothers had joined Tucker on the project of seeing what was in the large metal barn. They'd unearthed the Halloween items, too, he was happy to see. Caleb and Harlin were seeing if they were usable. Even Harlin's kids were helping as much as they could. Actually, it looked to him like they were more in the way than not, but he didn't care. It was a beautiful day, and he was enjoying life again.

"Did you read about your friend Parker's mom? His family is having a large party. It's to celebrate his life. And from what I've read, he had a good one, too. He's nothing at all like his father and has, I guess, cooperated with the police, dealing with a lot of unsolved deaths that his father might have had a hand in. Also, his sons. They're making welcome. I don't know what that means to them, but that's what the newspaper is calling their policy on how things are being done now that Papa Parker is gone." He said that he'd seen it this morning, telling Martin that they were going to go to it too. "Do you think they'd mind if we showed up unannounced? I think it would be a blast just to watch people hanging out. I know that there will be good food there as well."

"I was going to extend the invite to you all anyway. That way, you can meet some of my new family at the same time that I do." Joey asked if the will had been read as yet. "Not yet. With Parker's mom dying just after he did, there were a lot of things that had to be taken care of first. Mostly, I think that it's finding a venue for the two services. Then, after that, the funeral itself. There will be a great many people that want to lookee-lookee." Sebastian pulled out a large trunk and sat it on the ground. "This one says that it has books in it. Do you think we should start making piles of things in order? I know that the library is empty of books right now, and these might fill in the spaces."

"Excellent idea." After getting organized with where things were going, things seemed to flow much better. There was a lot to sort through, too. Years of stuff from several generations had been stored here. "What's in this one? It has two marks on it. Books, then toys. Do you suppose it's the trucks that are for Kelly?"

They decided to put those things, double-marked or not marked at all, closer to the house. Whatever happened to be in them would be sorted out later. However, as it turned out, there were three trunks and several boxes that held toys. Some of them belonged to Toby if he didn't miss his bet.

They weren't your everyday girly kind of things either. There was a chemistry set as well as blocks made of solid wood. He thought that James might have played with them, too, but he knew in his heart that they belonged to Toby. He didn't find much in the way of dolls, just one that he thought was an heirloom. He put that aside out of harm's way so that he could ask her about it later.

Everything that they'd pulled out and opened looked like it had just been put away. Even the trucks, older than even Toby, it seemed, were in great condition. He was stacking the things up in a way that he could carry them into the house when they were finished when Toby called them all in for lunch. Sebastian was surprised to find that the other wives were there as well with the kids.

"We thought we'd have a nice fun afternoon with the kids. They can break in the toys for Kelly and have something to do as well." The shelves were cleaned off for the books in the large library, and each of them brought in a couple of the trunks to be put away. The ladies were going to do that, and he couldn't have been happier with the turnout. Even Tucker was getting into bringing memories back into the old house. "How's it going out there?"

"Great, actually. We're organizing the boxes that we know we want to keep close to the house. Mostly, that's decorations for the yard. And Caleb had a great idea in hiring the local kids to put the decorations up for us. There are a great many Christmas ones. Most of which I think work." Toby looked like an excited kid to hear that. "Caleb and Tabby want to host Thanksgiving this year, and I volunteered us for Christmas. I hope you don't mind."

"No, not at all. I think that's wonderful. Do you know if any of them do traditional things?" He said that the only one that he knew had ever celebrated Christmas was Caleb. "That's sad. So we'll have to go all out on this, including the kids. We'll make it our first Christmas together as a family. I wonder if Daniel will make it here by then. He's still being looked for, correct?"

"Last I heard, there wasn't a home where his last address was. Caleb did some research, and it turns out that the apartment building had been condemned long ago, and they finally tore it down. They did give vouchers to the people living there, but no one picked up Daniels. With the voucher, they were supposed to give their new address. However, since he didn't pick his up, that left them without a forwarding. But he is still looking for him." Toby nodded, but he could tell she was distracted. "What is it you're thinking, honey? Anything that I can help you with? Or have someone else help you with?" Her laughter made him smile.

"No. I was just thinking about how hard this must have been on all of them. Being sired by the same bastard. Then, if that wasn't bad enough, all of them have had a terrible life but Caleb. I'm so glad that you made it here." He said that he was, as well. When the doorbell rang, he said that he had it. On his way there, he saw a large stretch limo in the driveway. "Oh, that's for me."

"You going someplace without me?" When she raced him to the door, he laughed. While he didn't have a clue what was going on, he was excited because she was. As soon as the doorbell rang, he stood stock still as he looked at the little girl standing there. "Daisy? My goodness. Look how much you've grown."

He couldn't have been more surprised than to find his little sister — well, the little girl he'd been told was his sister — standing on the front steps of their home. Hugging her just didn't seem enough, so he kept at it until they both pulled apart laughing.

"How did you —" He looked up at Toby. "You did this, didn't you? Brought her home for me."

"I brought her home for us. Caleb pulled a few strings for her, and we've adopted her. She and I have been getting to know one another on her trip here by way of cell phone. She's excited to have such a large family waiting for her. And a little brother." He hugged Toby tightly, too. "Take her in and —"

Daisy hugged Toby. Tightly too. When she went on bent knee to get a better hug, he called for his family to come and meet the newest family member. Sebastian couldn't believe that she'd done this for him and couldn't wait to show her around. His family was complete…for the moment, anyway. And he couldn't have been any happier than he was right this minute.

She went to pick out her room, and he wasn't surprised that she chose the one closest to Kelly's room. When she finally got to meet their son, she mothered over him like the two of them had been together forever. Once they were settled down and enjoying getting to know each other, he and the other men went out to the barn again to find what they could for the house. It was going to take them forever at the rate they were going right now.

By dark, they were finished with the barn. Mostly, it was just emptied out into the yard, but they had it all separated into neat piles of what went where. After bringing in all the crates and boxes that had *books* written on them, it didn't seem as daunting. But there were still lots of things to sort through, but now it was easier to get put away.

"You do know that there are two more barns like this one on the property, don't you?" He put his hand over her mouth and told her that they'd not get help if she told them. "I guess you're right. This calls for a celebration. Tomorrow night, let's have steaks on the grill for everyone."

"I love that idea." He did, too. After everyone left with the invite to come back tomorrow, it was Joey who suggested that they invite the extended family as well. Having them all together as a family was something that he loved even more. "We'll make it about five. That way, we can talk while the food is being readied."

In the end, it was decided that it was going to be too many people to have to cook for. So Toby made a few calls, and they were going to have some people come and cook for them. Also, she ordered side dishes to be made up, as well as someone to come in and clean up after they were done. Sebastian thought that was a much better idea anyway. They could visit with the family rather than running around messing with cooking duties.

~*~

"You'll be here for the reading of the will, right?" Sebastian looked confused, but Harold nodded. "You will be. Your name is mentioned in it as well."

"No, that can't be right. I only just met your father a few days before his death. Besides, I'm not sure what he'd have to say about me in the will." Harold told him that he was family. "I know, but only barely family. I don't need anything more than what I have right now. This is more than I could have hoped for when I went to see your father."

"Dad thought a great deal of you and Toby. You know that he was watching over you, so to speak, as you were growing up. It wasn't until later that he found out that you were related to us." He again told him that he was barely a relative. "Hey, we're a big, happy Italian family. The more, the merrier, is what Dad used to say. But you'll be there. Don't make me have to send someone for you, Sebastian."

"No. Okay, yes, I'll be there." David watched Sebastian as he moved around the family. He could see the things that his dad had told him about now. Sebastian carried himself well. He wasn't rude to people when they grabbed him and hugged him. Even when his overzealous aunts dragged him up from the table to give him hugs and kisses did he shy away from them. And he was quick to introduce the other side of his family to them as well. He would fit well into the family dynamics of this family.

Harold knew what his dad had done for Sebastian. He and his brothers had been sat down with their dad the morning before he had passed. Dad told them that he thought that since he'd missed out on the family, they should all make him feel welcome. That included having him be a part of the new enterprise that Dad had started. They were going to be a giving family from now on. And all three of them had agreed that his dad had it spot on.

At first, none of them wanted Sebastian to be anything but a blot on the ground when they'd found out that he'd turned down Dad on working for him.

No one had ever said no to him before and they were both shocked and pissed off about it. Then, the more that dad told them about the younger man, the more respect they had for him. Even walking across the United States to be with his brothers had impressed the hell out of him. Collin sat down next to him with a platter of fresh vegetables and fruit. They had all gotten on the bandwagon of eating healthier.

"Did you know that Momma Roman is leaving her sauce recipe to Toby?" He said that he'd heard that too. "I'm glad she didn't—" He looked around before continuing. "I'm glad that she didn't leave it to my wife. She would have tried but wouldn't have been able to pull it off. Not like she will."

"Do you think it might have occurred to someone that she might not cook?" Collin looked around again. "Not your wife, idiot, but Toby. She has a staff. I doubt that she spends any more time in the kitchen than Clara does."

"You think?" He nodded at his brother. "Nah, you're funning with me. Everyone wants to cook for their man. You know how momma did."

"You, my dear brother, are the reason that women hate Italian men. You're in the twentieth century. You are aware of that, aren't you?" He said he knew what year it was. "Yet you spout off things like women being in the kitchen. No wonder you and Clara are having trouble. Perhaps you should hang out at my house more. I know how to treat my wife."

"You spoil her." He said that he did, proud of the fact that someone noticed. "Did you know that your wife wants to go to college again? Why, I ask you? What does she need another education for?"

"Because she wants to learn all that she— sometimes I wonder if you weren't switched at birth. You are nothing like Cramton and I." He told him that he was glad for that. They were pussies. "Sure, you go on thinking that, and we'll see who has the best marriage. I'm about as happy as I can be, and my wife loves me. I don't have to sneak around corners to make sure that I don't have to spend time with my wife. Dork. What are you going to do when she decides that she could do better than you?"

"I could. I really could do better than her." Again, his brother looked around like he was terrified that his wife was nearby. "You really think that Toby doesn't cook? That would be really sad for Sebastian. Not having a homecooked meal to come home to."

"He's a stay at home dad." That got his brother coughing his carrot sticks all over himself. "Not only that, but he is richer than you are, thanks to his wife having more money than we do. Their combined worth is a great deal."

"Why? Why would you tell me shit like that when I'm eating. That's just sickening." When he finally told his brother to go away, he sat there watching the people interacting with each other. When his little girl joined him, she was going to be eighteen soon, he only just realized, he held her hand in his.

"I've been thinking about things. A lot. I don't want to go on the trip to Europe. I want to stay here and get to know the family, the newest family." He asked her if she'd spoken to her mom. "No. Not yet. I will, but I wanted to talk to you about it first. I wasn't very happy about it when it was mentioned at my sixteenth birthday party. I'm no more wanting to go now than I did then. It's just not me. I just don't know how to approach Mom about it."

"You do what you want, honey. Haven't your mom and I told you that all your life?" He wouldn't admit to her that he was relieved that she didn't want to go. The thought of his little girl traveling with a bunch of other girls her age alone bothered him to no end. "I know you have a plan, so why don't you tell your old man, and I'll help you out with telling your mom."

"Telling Mom what?" Vicky sat down next to their daughter, and it shocked him every time that she looked just like her mom did when she was the same age. Beautiful. "Is this about your trip? I've been thinking that you're not going to enjoy it as much as I thought you were. And if you're game, I was thinking that your dad and I could take you on the trip but not walking everywhere. I want comforts."

"Really? You'd want to hang out with me? This would be epic." When their daughter walked away, he smiled at Vicky.

"How did I become the luckiest man on earth? You, a lovely daughter, and you." She told him that he had said her twice. "Because I feel that I'm twice as lucky. How much did you hear before you pretended to come to this conclusion that we needed to take the trip with her?"

"All of it. I was hurt at first, I will tell you that. But after I heard her say that she didn't know how to approach me about it, I was more hurt by that. I thought that I could be the bigger man and just admit I wanted her to take this trip so that I could live vicariously through her. Then I realized, hey, we have money. We should just make a trip of it together."

He laughed while holding her hand. He did love this woman more than he did anyone in the world. As they sat there watching people, something that they both enjoyed more than anything, he told her what he and Collin had been talking about.

"Clara isn't happy in their marriage. She's not been for a long time. I don't know that it has all that much to do with Collin. More like she didn't get what she wanted in marrying into a mobster's family." He asked her what she had thought. "You remember that movie we watched the other night? The one where there were all kinds of stupid shit going on in the family that got them into trouble? Well, I think that's what she thought that she'd be getting into. You know, guns about the house all the time. Stashes of money all over the place. Not to mention the police coming around all the time wondering what her husband was up to. We don't have that sort of family."

"No. We don't. Thanks to Dad." She told him how much she missed him. "I do, too. So very much."

"What do you think we should do about it? I mean, as the head of the family now, you can have her taken out if you wish it." He stared at her for a full ten seconds before they both burst out laughing. "Christ, that was funny. No, but seriously, something needs to be done before she flies off the handle again. The last time nearly had Collin in prison. I don't know how he could stay with her after she had him arrested for things that he didn't do."

"I'll talk to him. Though it's doubtful that he'll

see what she did as anything more than just a cry for more money. He figures if he throws money at her, then she'll be happy. I don't think that's going to work." Harold was surprised when Toby sat down next to them. After telling them that she wanted to help, he asked her what she needed.

"I don't need anything. But have a feeling that you do. Did you know that Clara is telling people that your brother is having an affair? I hate to point this out, but he'd have to have his tongue ripped out— which might not be a bad thing—if he was to ever have a woman want to be with him, much less let him fuck her. He's a Neanderthal."

"He is at that." The three of them laughed as they kept an eye on Clara. "She's not going to be happy when I have a talk with her. What would you say to her? If you were to take this project for me."

"Say to her that you're head of the household now, and if she fucks up again by telling lies, I heard about her earlier trouble that you'll have her taken care of. You can mean that you're going to have her put in a home, but she won't care. You're being all mobsters-like. Anyway, I heard her telling my brother-in-law that she could make it worth his while if he were to fuck her. That is going to get her killed if Tabby finds out." Harold was shocked to his core that she'd say something like that to a guest. "There's more. Do you want to hear it?"

"Yes and no. But you'd better tell me. I don't want to have to have a clean-up without knowing all the facts." She told him her plan. Even looking at his wife, Harold could tell that she was impressed, too. "So we just pay her off to disappear. Will she stay away, you think? I don't want to have to pay her off over and over again when she runs out of money."

"She won't be back. It's not the money that she is in need of. It's someone recognizing that she's the injured party in all this." He asked her what she meant. "If you pay her off, and I'm talking not as much money as you're thinking, she'll be able to tell people that she was once in a mob's family and that they paid her off to go away. That and a one-way trip to someplace far away will give her a new crowd of people to listen to her and maybe take her seriously. Not too seriously, though. What do you think? Oh, by the way, did you know that Collin is terrified of her?"

"He isn't terrified of her but just doesn't like her." She handed him a sheath of papers. They were hospital bills, all with Collin's name on them as the patient. "Where did you get these?"

"I'm a very wealthy woman, Harold, and as such, I check out everyone that I have contact with. I have a husband and children. I want them to be safe. So when I found these, I figured that she was abusing her poor husband." She handed him another paper, this one filled with dates and times. "Those are to an underground abortion clinic. The very fact that they've only been married almost ten years, and these date back for as many as fifteen, tells me that she's not as faithful as she makes out to be. If it were me, I'd get rid of her right now. She's about to have another visit to the clinic."

Harold stood up, his blood boiling. But it was Vicky who told him to have a seat. She'd take care of this. The two of them watched as she made her way to his sister-in-law. Whatever went down, and he was sure that it was going to be huge, Vicky would handle it like a pro.

"I like you and your wife, Harold." He didn't take his eyes off his wife when he told Toby that he liked her too. "She took the paperwork with her. She's going to get rid of her without costing you a dime, I think."

When Toby left him, laughing her ass off as she did, he continued to keep an eye on his wife. He wasn't worried about her getting hurt. There were enough people around that Clara would be dead if she tried anything. Harold knew the exact moment that Clara knew she was caught.

Vicky pointed to the house, and then she looked like she was waving his brother over. Not Collin, but Cramton. After showing him the paperwork that Toby had given them, he took Clara by the arm and 'helped' her leave the party. He wasn't surprised to see that he took several men with him, too. Vicky came back to sit with him.

Not a word was spoken about Clara. They didn't bring up how they were going to tell his brother why she'd be gone when he got home either. And there was no doubt to him that there wouldn't be a trace of her left in the house by then either. Taking his wife's hand into his, he kissed the back of it and told her that he loved her.

"I don't think we should tell Toby that we owe her. I have a feeling that she'd make us regret it." He agreed with her and then laughed a little. "Yes, I think it's funny too that we're the head of what was once a large operation as a mob family, and we're terrified of offending a slip of a girl. Perhaps she should be in charge."

They were both still laughing about it when some of the crowd started to leave. Even later in the evening, when it was just him in the living room, he would get a chuckle out of Toby and them being afraid of her. Not that he wasn't. He was just a little, and he'd make sure that the family knew not to fuck around with her from now on.

Chapter 7

Cassie didn't want to stay at work another moment longer. However, since she'd only just arrived at seven and it was only seven ten, she was going to have to stay. Pouting to herself, she logged onto her computer and began pulling up requests that were sent to her overnight. Forty-seven emails was a bit much, but she knew that it wasn't the most she'd ever received working for Adler Real Estate.

"What are your plans for next week? You're on vacation, right?" She said that she was, but she wasn't going to tell anyone her plans. "You're afraid they'll cut you off again? I would be, too. How many times have they done this to you? Five? Six?"

"Eight. But this time, I'm being smart. I have all the paperwork approved and copies made so that I'm not going to be here." She would quit. Enough was enough, and her kind of skill wasn't something that everyone could do. "I'm going to be gone most of the day today. If you hear anything, will you let me know?"

He wouldn't. Jack was a follow around the boss with his nose stuck up his ass kind of employee. She had also learned that if she wanted the office to know anything, just tell him. Jack was a bigger gossiper than anyone she'd ever known. Even her mom wasn't as good as he was. And at least her mom was upfront about spying on people to get the juicy stuff. Jack would just as soon stab you in the back than to miss anything going on around the office.

It was why no one knew where she lived. They thought they did. But she'd been out of her old place for over three years now, and no one was the wiser. Cassie even had a post office box set up in a different town that would funnel her mail to her once a month when she made the arrangements with the boss there. She had a lot of people owing her a favor, and it had worked out well for her.

Making sure that she had all her equipment before leaving the office, she made sure every time that she also had her badge, cell phone, as well as lots of thumb drives. No one owned her work but her. Not until she was paid. It was in her contract as well, as she made sure that every house she worked with also knew that she owned the rights, not the agency nor the boss.

Cassie enjoyed her job. It got her out of the building every day, and she got to see some really cool things while filming. She'd been approved by the FAA, the Federal Aviation Administration, to fly her unmanned aerial vehicle, or UVA, so she used it to record views of houses for sale that no one else could get.

The roof, a good shot of the yard and how close or not they'd be to their neighbors. Even how dense trees might be or how overgrown it might have become while waiting on a buyer. She didn't hold back on the filming either. If she had been asked to cover a property, they got all of it. And for a lot more money, she'd record the inside of the house as well. That took a lot of time and work to get through a house with one of her smaller drones. Especially if it was still occupied.

She was on her third house of the day when she took a break. Cassie didn't usually stop for lunch or breakfast until about two. Today was no different. However, it was hotter than hell, and she was about as dry as she'd ever been. Pulling out a bottle of water from her backpack, she looked around the yard she'd just finished filming.

It was a shitty backyard. It looked like, at one time, it had had an inground pool that someone got the bright idea to fill in with dirt. They'd not bothered with taking up the concrete walkway around it, so it stuck out like a sore thumb. Cassie didn't think that they'd used good dirt either to fill it in. More like bags of thrash then that were filled in with dirt they might have dug up in other parts of the yard. It would take more to make the yard livable than it would to remodel the whole house. Just as she was set to get back to work, her cell rang. It was her brother.

"I have nine questions for you." She laughed and asked him if they were in any particular order or would he ask them one at a time. "What? You know what, never mind. I need you to do me a favor, too. I'll talk to you about it when we're finished here."

"You do know that I'm working, don't you?" Bradley asked her if she was too busy for her favorite person. "I don't know. He's not called me today, so I guess I'll have to help you."

"Very funny. Where are you anyway?" She told him and then told him he had only eight more questions. "As it so happens, that was one of my questions. I'm coming to you. One of the things that I need an answer for is something that you need to see."

While waiting for Bradley to come to her, he'd be on his bike, so it wouldn't take him long she finished up the yard. That was all there was for her to do as the rest of the house she'd finished up before the yard.

She was packed up and waiting by her car when he pulled in behind her. As soon as he was within talking distance, he started talking like they'd never had a twenty-minute break from their original conversation.

"You see this mess here? I don't know what I'm looking at. Tell me what you see, and that might help me." She took the laptop from him and watched the recording that he had. After telling him what it looked like to her, he took the computer and messed with it, then handed it back again. "What is that if the other thing was the door and window on the recording? Is that another entrance to the house? Or did someone, you, in this case, get too much of the neighboring home so that I can't see what I want?"

"You know, I never mess up. But yes, that is the neighbor's door. If you remember, I told you that the house next door was abandoned and that I thought that they were using it as a way to get in and out of both homes. See how it has that flashing over the walkway between them. From the aerial view, you don't see it. It's like there is nothing there the way they have it set up. A person could go between the houses with a camera right on top of the two doors, and no one would be the wiser. Why is this an issue now? That was four years ago." He told her. "Oh. I hadn't read anything about that. I'm sorry."

"You don't read any news, little sister, and that is why it's good that you have me in your life. The houses are being used again for drug drops. The people go into one house, pay up, then four hours later, they come back to the other house on the pretense of getting pizza or some shit delivered, and that's where they get their order. I believe that it's hidden either on the person or in the hot bags that they all seem to have now. I told my boss that both houses needed to be torn down. Now, he wants me to figure out how to stop this from happening again. Bastard."

Bradley was an agent with the local FBI. She had been, too, at one time, both of them working together a great deal until she had her little nervous breakdown. Smiling to herself, she knew that it wasn't even close to being little. She'd been locked up for nearly six months before she was able to come back to herself and another year before she could function in life again.

"I could set you something up, but you'd need someone to approve the time. I have the equipment, it's just old stuff that I don't use anymore, but I'll do it if you want." He asked her how long it would take her. "Not long. A couple of hours at the most. More than likely, if I can get in there in the early morning, I can do it in less time than that. It's up to you."

"I'll see what I can do." While waiting for her brother to make the call, she packed up her things and was ready to go home until it was approved. Bradley would know that she'd need it in writing that verbal anything wasn't going to fly with her. "He said for me to come by the office later, and he'll have the paperwork all filled out." When he frowned, she waited for him to tell her. When nothing was forthcoming, she punched him in the arm and told him to say to her. Bradley was more closed mouth than she was.

"He agreed, don't get me wrong, but he wants me to come by right now and get the paperwork for you to work on it. He procrastinates his piss time until he nearly wets his pants. This isn't right." She told him that she'd do it on her own time. "Good. I was hoping that you'd say that. I told him that I had a date tonight and that I'd already picked up my girl. Wanna get some dinner with me? That way, when I have to meet up with him tomorrow, I can honestly say what I had to eat."

"Sure, but you're buying this time. I'm still waiting on a couple of checks, and you know that I won't dip into savings for anyone." They were both laughing when he got on his bike. "We'll meet at your house?"

Kathi S. Barton

"No." She stopped getting into her car when he snapped like that. She didn't know what he was talking about until he fell off his bike. Turning to see what was going on, she had just enough time to drop behind her car door before shots were being fired. "Cassie, come get me."

She pulled out her weapon, firing at the car when it paused at her brother's bike. He was trapped beneath it, and it terrified her when she stood up to fire at the car. She wasn't sure if he'd been hit or not, but she knew that she would give her life to save him.

When the car took off, they fired at her instead of Bradley. She took a deep breath before going to his side. After two tries, she was able to get his bike off him and pulled to her car before she looked at him. There was some blood on his face but nothing that seemed life-threatening. It wasn't until he pulled open his jacket that she could see that he'd been shot.

"You know what to do." She nodded, not looking at him. He jerked her face up to hers and told her again. "Make the call, Cassie. They were gunning for me. I need to make sure that you're safe."

Going to her car, she pulled up the mat in the back from the floor and opened the safe that was there. The entire time she was doing this, she went over every step they'd been taught since they were children.

Make the call. No matter what, make the call. As soon as she was able to press the button without dropping the phone again, it was answered.

"Where are you?" She gave the operator the address where they were. "One or two pickups?"

"Two, same address. One injured." She was then asked if it was life-threatening. "Yes. GSW to the abdomen. Superficial wounds to face and hands."

"Five minutes. Code is Harvey the Rabbit." She laid the phone on the ground after taking out the SIM card and then destroyed it. Going back to her brother, she took his phone too and did the same thing to his and his burner. Things were about to hit the fan, and she didn't have any idea what was going on right now.

In three minutes, a white van pulled up beside her car. Bradley was loaded in the back of it and was being worked on. She was put in the front seat, and they were tearing away from the scene when she felt the wave of heat when the house she'd been filming simply blew up in flames. Her car, as well as his bike, would be a part of it. The two bodies that had been in the van when it pulled up also would look like she and her brother had been killed in the gas leak.

Dental records would be matched, and for all intents and purposes, Cassandra Blake and Bradley Benson would be dead. And they'd be given a new identity as well as another job and home to live in for a while. Christ, she hated her life. But they were alive, and she supposed that was enough for them.

~*~

Daniel looked over the paperwork again. Caleb Anderson was making too many waves for him to ignore. He was going to have to go and see what the man wanted, and soon, before he took too many more steps into finding him. He had a delicate balance right now and was afraid that someone other than him got hurt. He didn't want it to be Caleb or the other men that he'd claimed as family.

"Danny, what do you know about a house explosion on Dewy Street?" He said that he hadn't heard anything. "House and two victims destroyed. The only thing that they do know for sure is that the neighbors, about three miles away, said they smelled gas. Would they be able to smell it from that far?"

"I suppose so." He put his paperwork back in his drawer and turned to the kid who was supposed to be his assistant. The only thing he'd been able to assist him with was a migraine from hell and annoying the fuck out of him. "Have you sent anyone out there yet? To see if it's true or not?"

"I should do that, huh?" Daniel didn't bother telling him that he should have sent someone the moment he heard the rumor. "I'll send out a crew."

"You do that, moron." As he was picking up his paperwork again, putting all his things into his briefcase, Daniel was sort of sad that this was going to be his last day. Doing undercover work for the Bureau was fun most of the time, but he'd learned a great deal about small-town news organizations by being here for the last four months.

Sending off his report, he was putting his things in his car when he saw the firetruck race by him. Must have been true, he thought as it was headed toward the little street that had been mentioned. Pulling out into the little bit of traffic, he was nearly into the street when a full-sized white van pulled in front of him. Putting his hand on his weapon, he waited to see what was going on.

"Doctor Watson, I presume." The man laughed, and Daniel rolled his eyes. He said that he'd been wanting to say that for months. "I have a male in here that is in need of your help."

"What sort of help?" He was getting into the van's back doors when someone got out on the other side and got into his car. A medical team of two was in the van with the man, and he could see that he'd been shot. "Do we have a place to work from?"

"Yeah, we're headed there now. Hang on." He

did. Knowing this particular driver as being a full on idiot, he watched as the man's blood pressure was being taken. Then, when they were stopping at what he assumed was a stop light, he had a chance to look at the wound and assess it. "Four minutes."

In less time than that, he was cutting the man open and removing the bullet. While he was being stitched up by the med team, he gave the man something for infection and pain after ascertaining that he'd not been given either in the few minutes that he'd been in the van. Christ, this kid must be important if—

"Cassie? Cassie? Christ, she's bleeding too." They were in front of the house when she was scooped up and taken inside. The man would be taken care of as well, but he needed to see what he could do for the young woman. The bullet had entered her left shoulder and was still in there. Whoever had shot this couple, they had missed the spot twice. Hell was going to be paid. He'd bet anything.

It took him nearly an hour to get the woman to the point where he didn't think she was going to die. It had been touch and go there for a little bit. She had coded twice. Opening her chest up in a strange house without any precautions was the only thing he could do, as it turned out. The bullet had nicked her aortic artery, and she was bleeding internally. Lucky for her and him, the house had the equipment to keep her alive.

Sitting next to the two people, he didn't bother asking who they were. If they had wanted him to know, they would have told him by now. Instead, he looked over the paperwork that he'd brought with him when he'd gotten into the van.

"Did you find any misdealing's there?" His boss, FBI Director Charles Dow, sat down next to him in another chair. "Not that I don't think it could happen, but the town is just too…I don't know, Disney-like for there to be foul play there."

"You'd think that, wouldn't you. But no, I didn't find that any of the allegations were true. The newspaper is above reproach, and they have a good community thing going on, too. It's just like you said, very Disney-like." Daniel got up and checked on the female. "I down know that you're going to tell me anything, but these two were from there, right? Her clothing had a real-estate name on them, and he was dressed like you. What gives, if I can ask?"

"She is Cassie, Cassandra Blake. FBI. You might have heard about her when her husband was murdered right in front of her. Then the man is her brother, Bradley Benson. He does work for us, too." He asked if she was the one who had had the nervous breakdown.

"That's her. She's been working for us under the guise of video surveillance for the realtor by the name of Alder. I'm not sure how much either of them knows about what happened today, but they were leaving a job when someone opened fire on the two of them. As you were able to figure out, she'd not known that she'd been shot until she was in the van. They're tight, the two of them."

"Okay, that explains who they are, but what are they? I'm assuming since everything moved so quickly that they're important in some way." He only nodded. "Okay, closed-mouthed. I'm all right with that. It was my last day at the newspaper office anyway. Can you at least tell me where I'm headed next?"

"Yes. You're not going to like it." He looked at the people in the beds and then back at his boss. "I need someone to watch over them until they're healed enough to take care of themselves. And I have the perfect spot for you to do it. You get to meet up with your long-lost family, too."

"Caleb Anderson." Charles nodded. "Why him? I mean, there has to be a better place than a family member's home? Don't you have any safe houses that I could stay at with them? I mean, I'm not even sure that the two of us are related."

"You are. You're his half-brother." He took

the paperwork that was being held out to him. "You remember his mother, don't you? Abigail Anderson?"

"Yes." He did, too. Abby had been a good friend of his when— "She's his mother? Caleb is related to Abby Anderson? Christ, now I know why he's like this, not leaving shit alone when he couldn't find me. He's just like her."

"Thank you." The large man came into the room with him. There was no mistaking that they were related. When Caleb sat down, he looked at Charles. "He called me early last week when he found out that I've been looking for you. I had to pull a few strings to even get as much information that I had on you to come through. Then, about two hours ago, he called me again and told me that not only were you in town but that you needed me to help you. Welcome to the family, Daniel. We've all been waiting for you."

"Do you have any idea what we're doing here? Why I've been trying to avoid you? I'm an undercover FBI agent that is about as close to death as anyone gets on a daily basis who works with bad people. I could very well get your entire family killed." Caleb told him that they were his family, too. "Look, this is a bad idea. I don't know these two people here, but they've been targeted to be killed, and the kind of people that do that sort of shit in broad daylight won't give a shit if you have six or six hundred people protecting you. They'll plow through you like you're nothing." Charles got up and left them there. It was then that he looked at his half-brother when he laughed.

"We have help." Daniel got up and started to pace. "My mother, she knew about you. I found some information about you that I didn't with the rest of them. Just notes on things. How you became so good at your job. She said that you have an ability that no one knows about."

Daniel stopped pacing and turned to look at the other man. Then he looked around to see if anyone had heard. While he knew that the room was being recorded, it wouldn't get shit while he was there. Not any mikes, cameras, or cell phones would work. It's why he didn't carry one. Nor wear a watch.

"What did she tell you? I've not seen her in a long time. How is she doing?" Caleb told him that she had passed away seven months ago from cancer. "Oh, I'm so sorry. She was a brilliant woman and one that I loved more than my own mother at times. I didn't know. I had no way of — You have my deepest condolences, Caleb. She was a wonderful woman."

"She was. And she made me promise that I'd find all my brothers. You were the last one." Caleb laughed. "You'd not believe the shit that we've gone through with each of them. Sebastian was the last to join us before you had a mobster after him. Whatever we need to do, Daniel, to keep you safe, we're going to get through it. I promise."

He didn't bother telling him that it wasn't good to make promises like that when he didn't know what was going on. It was like the brother and sister that he was watching over now. Who knew what sort of shit was going to come about with having them around too.

"It's going to be hell. I hope you understand that." Caleb said that he'd been told it was going to be the worst yet. "That's about as accurate as it can get. I've been in and out of places that would make your hair turn white, as the saying goes."

They talked for the next hour. Not on any kind of plan to get them to his home. Not about what might be coming after the two on the beds with all kinds of shit hooked up to them. Caleb told him about his wife and brothers. The children and what they were up to. How his grandparents were helping out with projects around town that he might have heard of.

Daniel was impressed. All the good works that were going on around town were something that Caleb had a hand in. He'd not even realized that they were in the same town until today. All he'd had to of done was walk down the street from the building he was working in and found his brother. Christ, talk about a small world. They had been together for the last few months, and neither of them knew a thing about the other.

When he was given a note, Daniel waited for him to read it before he let his tension go. Caleb looked at him, smiling when he handed him the note.

"Tabby is my wife. You'll learn not to mess with her. Or not. She'll love you anyway. But she's sort of firm about things. Well, you'll figure it out. She said that the basement has been converted into your lab of sorts and that you should come home with me and the other two." He asked him where he was going to be staying. "With us. Everyone in town knows that I've been looking for you. Most of the people won't even equate you with the man at the newspaper office. You didn't get out much, I'm to understand."

"No. I was working." Caleb stood up. "We're going now? To your home? I mean, this is a huge undertaking. How will you get the young couple there into your home?"

"It'll be a piece of cake." He wished he had the confidence that Caleb had. He'd never had an easy move in all his life and was sure that this wasn't going to be any different. Going out to the garage, he started laughing when he saw the setup that was going on.

Yes, he thought, it was going to be a piece of cake with this man in charge.

Chapter 8

"Mister, I'm not coming down outta this tree until you swear to me that that cur dog is out of sight. He already done did bite me once. I don't like donating my blood to nobody, especially not cur dogs." Daniel let himself laugh at the little boy in the tree. "You just go on now, Mr. Sebastian, and I'll be fine and dandy."

"Can I help?" Daniel had yet to meet any of the others but Caleb as his family, so he put out his hand to Sebastian, a man who could be his twin. "I think that we're brothers."

"You don't know that you're brothers? Sheesh, Mister. I got me five sisters, and they make for sure that everyone knows that they're related to me. They're all bigger and older than me, too." The little boy looked at him. "Yeah, I can see that you're his brother, so don't be thinking nobody else is gonna notice it."

"I didn't get to meet him when I came to town

yesterday. We all have the same father, but we've not been together before." Luke, he found out the boy's name and said that was nice for them all. "I guess. Where is the cur dog?"

As if he'd summoned the pooch, he came barking at them from around the corner. As soon as Sebastian told him to lay down, it did. Daniel was trying to hold back his laughter when Luke told the other man that he only minded big people, not little kids with teeth holes in his leg.

"He thinks you smell good to him." Luke told him that wasn't helping. "No. I suppose not. I'm not saying that you did anything, but could he have a reason for wanting to chomp on your legs? I mean, he doesn't look to me like a mean dog."

"I had to do it. My momma," Luke looked at Sebastian, then back at him before continuing again. "She's having herself a bad day. Dad, he knocked her around a bit and took all the money in the house again. I'm not asking for money, Mr. Sebastian. I'm just telling this man here, your brother, why the dog hates me. I was feeding him, you see. Putting out the scraps for him to munch on. You don't know what he looked like before I started doing that. All his ribs were fighting to be on the outside of his skin rather than where they're supposed to be. But momma, she got it in her head that we couldn't feed a cur dog—I don't even know what that means—no more on account of dad taking all the food money. Again."

"Is your momma all right?" Luke told him that she was in the hospital with his sisters. "All right. We'll come back to that. This dog, he's usually friendly to you, is he?"

"He is. Sometimes, when it's raining out, I bring him into my room and hide him away. My daddy, he'd have himself a conniption if he were to hear about that part. Woo Eee doggie. I'd be hurting." Daniel was having so much fun that he didn't want to leave, so he said he'd help the little boy and dog out. "The dog don't need much in the way of help, mister. He just needs to not be chomping on the hand that feeds him."

"Do you think perhaps you smell like your dad, and he's smelling him instead of you?" Daniel looked at Sebastian while Luke was thinking things over. "I was looking for Caleb and Tabby. I need to talk to them about something important. Do you know where they might be?"

"I know where Tabby is. She's with the other women out looking for a building to have the school's fair days in. They're just down the street at City Hall getting permits and standards that they're going to need." He asked about Caleb. "He should be with Joey.

That's the last place I knew anything about either of them."

A thick jacket hit him on the head, and he looked up at Luke. "That's my daddy's. He said he wanted me to drop it off to be dry-cleaned. I put it on so that I'd not lose it. You think that's all it was, Mister?" He said the only way to find out was to test it on the dog. "I'm not going to be happy if you've been funning with me about this. He already bit me once today."

Once Luke was out of the tree, he could see how badly the boy had been knocked around, too. Telling him to put his hand out to the dog earned him a look, but he had confidence in the plan that he'd laid out for him.

The dog was growling at the back of his throat, but he did inch his way to Luke. Almost as if he would have given up, the dog jumped into the little boy's arms and was trying to lick his face off. The giggling little boy and the happy pup were just what he needed right now.

"Now that he's not going to chomp on you anymore, do you mind if I have a look at your wound? I don't want him to lose you again because you got an infection." Setting the two of them on the sidewalk, he cautiously looked at not just the superficial bite mark but also as many wounds on his arms and legs as he could. "I think we should all pay a visit to the hospital to make sure you're up to date on your shots. We can check on your mom and sisters while we're at it."

"You a doctor or something?" He said he was a doctor. "We sure could use a doctor in my family. Dad comes around with his fists, all ready to do some hurting, and you could patch us up. Momma gets the most beating around. So does Serenity, but she hits him back now so he don't mess with her too much. Momma would too. She used to anyways. But since she's got the cancer, it's hard on her to defend herself." Luke looked up at the two of them. "I don't know what I'm going to do if I lose her. She's the best momma there ever was."

"She sounds like it." They took a hand each, and the three of them, with the dog following right behind, walked down the street. Sebastian said he had parked his car down here when he'd seen Luke up the tree. That was when he saw Caleb. "I have to talk to Caleb for just a minute. Do you think you guys could wait for me to go with you? I'd like to have a couple of tests run while — just give me a few minutes."

He was prepared for the bear hug that he'd gotten every time he came upon Caleb. It was breathtaking, literally, as well as it really did make him feel quite a bit better about things in general. However, he didn't have good news this time, and he almost hated to let him go.

"I heard about it." Nodding, he told him he was so sorry. "I am as well. While they didn't give us any kind of information on the two of them, it's still tragic that they both passed away. The young woman, Cassie, she had lost a lot of blood, you said, and the young man, Bradley, he was hurt pretty badly."

"If you don't mind me asking, how did you know?" He told him that his butler had gone to check on him and had heard him talking to someone about it. "I guess I could have been more discreet about it. I'm sorry that you had to find out that way. While I didn't really hold out much hope for the young woman, as you said, she'd lost a great deal of blood. I did hope for the young man to make it."

"Do you know what happens now?" He said that they'd make arrangements to have their bodies picked up for them. "No. I mean, I'm glad that is going to be taken care of. I meant about their killers. Do you know anything about if they've found them or not?"

"Several factions are taking credit for the deaths, though they don't say who they killed or where, so we're not putting much out there on that. I know that the president has his best men working on finding them. It happened on our soil, and he'll make sure that doesn't happen again. The two of them, brother and sister, from what I've been able to figure out, have lost a great deal in working for the government. I guess we'll just have to wait and see what else comes to us about it. I just don't know."

"Thank you for telling me." He got another hug. "You'll be staying, right? I mean, you just got here, and I'd hate to lose you so soon."

"I'm retired. I mean, I was retired before I came here. It was an easy assignment so that I could get my last fifteen days so that I could have my full retirement." Caleb smiled. "That's not to say that I might not get called in for something on this. Being on the scene when it first happened is about all the help I've been able to give them. But I was first on the scene, and I'm not sure what that will mean for the president."

"I'll have a talk to him." Daniel laughed, but Caleb didn't. He was never sure about this man. He'd never play against him in any game of life or just a board game. He held himself out there like he didn't have a care in the world, but once you got to talking to him, you saw a whole other part of him that he thought very few people did.

Going back to where he'd left Sebastian and Luke, he got into the car with them. As they were headed to the hospital, he thought about being a part of this growing family. He knew about Caleb and the others. Much more than he thought that they did about each other, and he was afraid that someone or something might happen to them. They were, he'd come to discover, just as friendly and nice as he'd read about them.

They pulled into the lot and went inside to the emergency department. There didn't seem to be a lot going on, but there were people waiting in the waiting room. A lot of them, about forty people. Daniel asked to see who was in charge.

"Nobody is." He didn't think that was right but asked again who was in charge of this shift in this department. "Are you deaf as well as stupid? Nobody. Fill out the paperwork over there on that kiosk thing and sit down. We'll get to you when we get to you."

He turned and looked at Sebastian, who looked as shocked as he felt. Going to the kiosk, he spoke quietly to Sebastian while trying to figure out how to handle this. He asked him if Caleb had any pull here.

"Yes. So does his grandparents. Want me—let me reword that. It would be my pleasure to call them and have them come here. The president of the hospital was terminated about a week ago. I don't have any idea what for, but I'm beginning to get a clearer picture now." Luke said he'd been turned away the other day when he'd come to see if his friend had broken his arm. "What happened to him?"

"He got himself an infection from the break, and they had to run him up to a bigger hospital. Sure is a shame, too. His family can't see him that far away." Daniel hadn't heard anything about the hospital around here. Not even working about as close to it as he had. He wanted to think that it was a one-time thing, but it was slowly becoming apparent that this was the norm for here. "You gonna get them in trouble? I hope that they don't know that my mom is in here. They'll take it out on her if they do. Or maybe she'll get better care. They been holding her pain stuff, Sen told me."

Enough was enough. Calling Caleb while Sebastian called Caleb's grandparents, he laughed when he heard that someone was calling in the wives. Just the little bit of time that he'd spent with Tabby, he knew better than to fuck around with her. She was the sweetest little thing, but she had a fire in her that could burn down a house at fifty paces.

Caleb showed up first. No one even blinked an eye when he asked who was in charge. They told him the same thing that they'd said to him. Nobody. This time, however, she sounded out each syllable like it was something she wasn't fond of repeating.

When the grandparents showed up, it was iffy

if they were going to be arrested. Mrs. Anderson was well up into the face of the woman behind the check-in counter, and she wasn't backing down, not even when security showed up. A sorrier bunch of men and women he'd ever seen, too.

After two more hours, he found himself sitting in the room of Olivia Branch. When Luke had said that his mother was dying, he hadn't mentioned that it might be as soon as today. It hadn't helped the woman to have been a punching bag for her husband, either. The daughters, five of them, were more protective of their mother and brother than he'd seen national security types protecting something.

"I don't have long, do I, Doctor?" He shook his head, and two of the girls stood up and dragged Luke along with them. "They're all I have in the world, and now I'm going to leave them to their father. Do you know of anyone who can take care of them for me? Just until my sister and Aunt can get here. I called them, but, well, money is tight everywhere. I was saving for them to send them money, but Burt took it all when he wanted to go and celebrate."

"What did he have to celebrate, Mrs. Branch, that was more important than your family having food on the table?" She said that he didn't pass that along to her, then laughed. "Luke takes after you in finding fun in about everything, I think."

"He's a good boy. Burt, he don't like him none because he's smart and corrects him all the time. Luke, he don't show off and talks like he's got not one brain cell in that noodle of his, but he's brilliant. Going to be ten next month and already done with high school. He's afraid his daddy will find out that he's really smart and make him find a job. My poor baby." The older daughter, Sen is what she went by, sat down on the other side of her mom and took her hand. "This one here, too, is brilliant. All of them are but Luke and Sen here, they've been the smartest of them all. Smart enough too that she won't marry anybody her daddy brings around because he said so."

"I don't live with them when he's home. I guess I thought that I could do more good than not if I had a job. I do, but it doesn't matter how much I bring to Mom and the others. Dad seems to know and takes it all." She told him that she was twenty-seven. "Though there are times when I feel like I'm twice that."

They talked to each other while Olivia dozed in and out. It really wasn't much longer for her to live. He'd been able to give her morphine to help with the pain, but she was almost too weak to do much more than moan. His heart broke for the little family, and he felt like he needed to do more.

What that would be wasn't anything that he could put his finger on. When Caleb showed up with food and the other kids, he helped Luke get his food loaded up on his plate and sit on the other bed. He ate with them as it had been a long time since breakfast, he told the little boy.

"Momma isn't going to come home this time, is she?" Daniel shook his head. "I didn't think so. She's worn out, isn't she? I don't want her to suffer anymore, but I don't want her to leave me either."

"She'll never leave you, Luke. Your mom will be with you for the rest of your life. She'll be watching over you. And every time you think of doing something you have to think hard on, you just ask yourself, what would my mom think if I did it this way. Or what would she do if she were in this place in my life? Every day, without her being right there beside you, you'll think about her, and she'll be right there guiding you." Luke hugged him, and he held him tightly while he thanked him for that. "You're so very welcome. I do the same with my mom every day, too. It's like she's my little angel right there on my shoulder, guiding me to do the right thing."

Luke held onto him for about twenty minutes before he realized that he'd fallen asleep. After he got him adjusted around so that he could lay him on the other bed, Alex helped him by covering up her brother.

"That's the nicest thing you could have done for him. He's been worried about that for weeks now, knowing that Mom was coming to an end. But you helped him. I can't thank you enough." He said that it had been his pleasure. "Doctor Watson, if you'd like to stay with us tonight here at the hospital, that would be great. Not as a doctor but as a friend. I think of you already as that."

"Yes, I'll stay."

~*~

Sebastian put the books away that he'd been looking at. It was nice having a good library at home. When he couldn't sleep, like tonight, he knew that he could go downstairs and pull out a book and be happy. He and Toby hadn't gotten a television yet, and he didn't know now if he wanted one. Until baseball season started, he supposed, but that was still a few months away.

"What's going on?" He turned and looked at Tucker and smiled. "You don't sleep much, do you? I usually see you a couple of times a night when I get up and empty myself out. Must have been hard on you as a youngster to not sleep well."

"Actually, I did sleep well as a kid. Not much, only about four hours a night, and I learned to hide myself away when my mom would come looking for me. She never put up much of an effort to find me, so it worked out well for me. I got to read a lot, and I think it helped me in my life to be able to sneak around quietly."

Tucker sat down on the couch and looked at him. He could tell there was something on his mind. It had been for the last couple of days. About the time that Daniel had shown up. Sitting down across from him on the other couch, he asked him what was going on.

"I've been thinking about that little boy and his sisters. Do you know who the father is?" He told him his name was Burt Branch. "Yeah, I thought that it might be him. Nasty sort of fella, he is. His daddy was worse, if you can believe it. Those little girls of his, you think that they're safe there at the hospital all alone?"

"Daniel is there with them. He called here earlier, telling Caleb that when he was here. Did you hear that Daniel can't use a cell phone? Strangest thing I've ever heard of." Tucker nodded, still distracted. "What are you thinking? If you want to go there and stay, I'll take you if you think it will make you feel better."

"I don't know what would make me feel better about them kids. I know two or three of them are adults, but that won't stop their father from hurting them if he wants to, does it?" Sebastian said that, sadly, it didn't. "Yeah, didn't think so either. How about me and you going there. Just to have a little look around. Maybe, if you don't mind none, we bring a few of them back here to rest up and shower. You been to their home? Ain't fit for a rat if you ask me. She tries, Olivia does. But there is only so much cleaning you can do to a house that will make it look brand new."

They were halfway there when he heard from Caleb. "Mrs. Branch died about half an hour ago. Daniel just called me. He's going to make arrangements for them to stay in a hotel." Sebastian said he was on his way there and he'd bring them to his home to stay. "That's a better solution anyway. Thank you for that. The little boy, I think you know him, he's taking it pretty hard. Also, if you'd not mind telling them, Burt is in jail. Drunk and disorderly. He'll be out in a couple of days. But for now, they can have a little bit of peace."

Sebastian helped Tucker and Daniel gather up some things from the house to be able to wear over a few days. There wasn't much. Caleb had been right. While the house was clean and smelled that way, too. It was just too old to get everything to be perfect. Sen, the oldest daughter, had some clothing in her car for her mother to use when the funeral home was ready for them.

The other women came to their home and, with the help of Toby, were getting the family settled in.

Daniel took care that Luke was all right and, in the end, gave him just a little of something to help him rest. Luke was both terrified of his father coming around and being alone with him. Daniel had brought Orange, the dog, with them and asked if he could sleep with Luke.

"Yes, of course. That's a good idea. Someone he can cuddle with." Daniel laid the dog by the little boy, and he wrapped his thin body next to Luke. "I think that they'll be good together, the two of them."

"Thank you for allowing him to come in. Most people wouldn't have allowed it." Sebastian said he wasn't like most people. "I don't think that anyone in this family is like anyone else in the world."

They both laughed, but when Daniel yawned for the third time, the two of them parted ways. He was going to stay here too and didn't mind at all that they were filling out the house with family. Picking up Kelly when he was fussing, he sat down in the rocker and told him everything that was going on while he took his bottle.

"We have a houseful of family. Well, it's not technically family, but it's close enough. They're going to eat you up tomorrow." He wondered if that was scary to his son and figured he'd have to get used to the way people talked around here. "Luke is going to love seeing another little boy, I think. He is a little overwhelmed by having so many little mommas, as he called them. He's a wonderful kid. You'll like him."

Even after giving him his bottle and burping him, he held his son and talked to him. It was a good way, he thought, to let his mind clear out. Not that he'd do that often; he didn't want his son to think that he was nutty, but for now, it soothed them both.

"Mr. Sebastian?" Turning from the baby bed after lying Kelly down, he smiled at the little boy. "I have Orange with me. Is that all right if we come in and see the baby? I promise you that we won't hurt him."

"Of course, it's all right. Come on, and I'll lift him up so you two can see him." Picking Kelly up from the bed, he opened one eye to look at the new strangers in his room. When he looked at Luke, both eyes wide with curiosity, the dog licked both their faces. "It looks like he's been given a big kiss."

He was surprised that Kelly didn't cry. Lying him on the floor so that both the dog and Luke could see him had Kelly smiling so brightly. When he took Luke's finger into his tiny hand, he thought for sure that Luke was going to have a heart attack. He seemed so delighted by the small move that Sebastian knew he was going to hug the little guy more when he saw him.

After it was apparent that Kelly had had enough, he put him back in his crib. Luke and Orange seemed disappointed, but Sebastian told them they could hang out with him tomorrow. Just as he suspected, the real reason that Luke had come to him was that he was missing his mom.

"Come on, little man. It's bedtime." Sen came out of the bedroom closest to where Luke was staying and smiled at him. "Why don't you go in there and get into my bed, and I'll read you some stories. I found an old chemistry book down in the library that we can go over and find all the mistakes they made back then. All right?"

"Sure. Thanks, Sen." When he disappeared into the room, she turned to him. Just as Luke popped his head back out, she looked like she was going to be upset. "Thanks for letting me see your baby, Mr. Sebastian. He's a cute guy." Then he closed the door behind him. Sen looked at him again.

"I need a job. All of us do, really. And we took a vote. None of us are going back to the house. It should have been torn down a long time ago, but it was Mom's house before Burt came along, and that's where they stayed." He said he'd not realized that the house wasn't a rental. "No. Mom owned it when I was born. Burt isn't my dad. He's the other's father, just not me.

I think that's why he disliked me so much. Anyway, I lost my job by coming here and trying to help my mom. So if you know of anyone hiring, will you let me know?"

"Of course. I think that you'd have better luck finding something if you were to talk to Caleb. Or Tabby. They seem to have the pulse of the town right at their fingertips." Toby came down the hall then, and he explained to her what was going on. "You know of any job openings, honey?"

"Yes, I do. I have four jobs that I have to fill that have to do with sorting clothing. I went by the donation house today and was blown away by the mess. I guess the lady who used to run it had too many rules about getting things and turned a lot of people off from trying to get something. If you could help me get them sized and separated, that would help a great deal. I don't know what her deal was about only letting people take ten things from the place a week. Christ, it's not like she had to pay for it." Sen told her that they'd gone there once, and she tried to tell them that since they were a family, they could only take ten things. Not each, just ten things. "For five girls and one boy? She thought that it was going to help you? No wonder there is so much in there that it's difficult to get around in the place. Once we get them all sorted, I'm going to get some machines put in so that they can be washed and dried right away. A lot of people around here don't have machines but have to carry things to the laundry mat daily. I'm glad someone called me and let me know what was going on. If I had known sooner, I would have taken over then. But you and your sisters, you'll help out?"

"Of course. Mom's funeral needs to be paid for, too. There just wasn't enough money for anything extra when she was so ill." He hurt for the family. And was ready to say that he'd pay for it when she spoke again. "I'm not asking for money here. I know that you and your family are wealthy enough to pay for it and make sure that we have nice clothing to wear. And someday, I might ask for help. But for now, I'm working on trying to keep my family together and learning to take care of themselves. All but Luke, anyway. He's too young to have much of a job, but we'll all take care of him."

"I've no doubt that any and all of you will do a good job in taking care of each other from now on. As I said to you earlier, your father, or I guess Burt, is in jail, so we'll make plans after tomorrow to keep you all safe. That's going to be something that we can all help you with." Nodding, she turned back to the bedroom when Toby spoke again. "Sen, if you need something, anything, let us know. I don't want any of you to do without when we have been so fortunate in having a little more. All right?"

"Yes. I understand. I want you to know that I might well need your help with things. But right now, I'm just wanting to be there for my family and get through this together."

When they made their way to their room, he held Toby while she spoke about the donation building. He knew that she was thinking of the Branch family, and he loved that she wanted to step in and take over. But she wouldn't. Not until asked. He thought that it was the bravest thing he'd ever seen his new wife do. Stepping back until asked. He supposed they'd see what tomorrow would bring and all the tomorrows after it. But he had a feeling, a small one yet, that everything was going to work out just fine. Just fine indeed.

AWARD WINNING, BESTSELLING AUTHOR

Kathi Barton, a winner of the Pinnacle Book Achievement Award and a best-selling author on Amazon and All Romance books, lives in Nashport, Ohio, with her husband, Paul. When not creating new worlds and romance, Kathi and her husband enjoy camping and going to auctions. She can also be seen at county fairs with her husband, an artist and potter.

Her muse, a cross between Jimmy Stewart and Hugh Jackman, brings her stories to life for her readers in a way that has them coming back time and again for more. Her favorite genre is paranormal romance, with a great deal of spice. You can visit Kathi online and drop her an email if you'd like. She loves hearing from her fans. aaronskiss@gmail.com.

Follow Kathi on her blog: http://kathisbartonauthor.blogspot.com/

www.ingramcontent.com/pod-product-compliance
Lightning Source LLC
Chambersburg PA
CBHW030223180626
46810CB00008B/2942